Triple Ψ Creek

Ranch

Book Two

Home at Last

Rebekah A. Morris

Copyright © 2014 Rebekah A. Morris

All rights reserved.

ISBN: 1494959488
ISBN-13: 978-1494959487

Read Another Page Publishing

DEDICATION

To Elizabeth Johnson whose eagerness and excitement to read the second book made me want to finish it quickly.

CONTENTS

Chapter 1

MATHEMATIC MISERIES

A chilly breeze blew in the open kitchen door causing Jenelle to pull her shawl closer about her shoulders. It was early November and winter was rapidly approaching. Already there had been heavy frosts and only that morning Lloyd Hearter had ridden in from a far pasture and said that Crystal Creek had a skin of ice.

Hearing the sound of crutches behind her, Jenelle turned and smiled as Norman made his way to stand beside her. It had been a month since his accident, and he was restless. It had been all the doctor, Mrs. O'Connor, Jenelle and Hardrich, Triple Creek's foreman, could do to keep Norman from leaving his bed too soon.

"Has Lloyd worked Minuet today?" he asked, looking over towards the barn and corrals.

Jenelle shook her head. "No, he was out by Crystal Creek this morning and then Hardrich sent him in to town."

"Then I think I'll go give her a little exercise."

"Norman Mavrich, you'll do no such thing!" Jenelle exclaimed, catching his arm. "Dr. French said you were not to get up on a horse until he gives you leave. Besides, you couldn't even saddle her."

"Darling, you could help me saddle her, and Minuet isn't going to throw me. It was last week that Doc said that. My leg is better now. Besides," he added, a restless look in his

1

eyes, "I've got to do something! Jenelle, this inaction is growing unbearable! And Minuet needs to be ridden. Hearter was too busy yesterday to do it."

Snatching a warmer cloak from beside the door, Jenelle said, "Well, if she needs to be ridden, I'll ride her. You follow the doctor's orders."

Seeing that his wife really intended to ride the pretty chestnut, Norman followed her outside protesting, "Jenelle, you shouldn't be trying to ride that horse. Darling, I give in, I won't ride her."

Jenelle turned. "But you said she needed to be ridden."

"She does but—"

A bright whistle sounded from the barn and Scott, the ranch's official wrangler stepped outside. On seeing the two in the yard, he touched his hat as he greeted them. "Howdy, sir, Mrs. Mavrich."

"Hello, Scott," Jenelle smiled. "Are you and all the others terribly busy just now?"

Scott shook his head. "No, ma'am. A couple of the men just finished helping me with the horses, and Hardrich said we could knock off the rest of the day if we've a mind to. You need something done?" Scott, as well as any of the hired hands on Triple Creek ranch, was always willing to help the mistress of the ranch. Not only did she treat them with a politeness often neglected to the working class, but she was always interested in them and their lives.

"Norman said that Minuet needs to be worked today and Lloyd has gone into town. I'm afraid if someone doesn't do it, he'll try it himself."

Norman chuckled. "She's right. I'm growing mighty tired of these crutches and all this confinement."

Scott laughed. It was good to see Mr. Mavrich out of bed and almost himself once more. "I'd do it myself, sir, but I'm under Doc's orders as well." And he grinned. The stampede which had injured Norman during the fall round-up had also given Scott several broken ribs, and Dr. French, knowing how careless these ranchers and cattlemen could be on horseback, was giving his patients no opportunity to re-injure themselves before they had a chance to heal completely. "Alden could do it though."

"Do what?"

Norman turned his head and saw Alden coming with an easy stride from the bunk house.

"Will you take Minuet out and give her some exercise? Take her for a ride somewhere. Hearter couldn't get to it yesterday and isn't around today, I hear."

"Sure thing, Mr. Mavrich. I'll take care of that right now. I've been wanting to ride that horse and see how she goes. Lloyd praises her enough."

As Alden and Scott headed towards the corral, Jenelle laid a hand on her husband's arm. "You should be getting back inside," she chided. "You aren't even wearing a jacket."

Norman merely grunted. He wasn't cold and he longed to be back at work with the men instead of lying around the house feeling like a useless invalid. "Jenelle," he sighed, looking down at her with such a pitiful expression that she laughed merrily, "I don't think I can stand this inactivity much longer. I mean to have a talk with Dr. French the next time he comes out."

"Well, come along now or Mrs. O'Connor will be out after you, and you can be sure that she'd tell the doctor you weren't following orders."

"I'm coming." Norman shook his head dismally and gave a resigned sigh. It was no use to protest the doctor's orders to Mrs. O'Connor or Jenelle; they wouldn't listen; at least, he amended to himself, they wouldn't side with him. Mrs. O'Connor had told him, "Tut, man, to be sure and it's not a hard life yer livin' now with yer good wife waitin' on you and bein' up an' out of bed entirely."

She was right, and Norman admitted to himself that he had much to be thankful for. The accident could have resulted in much greater damage to life than it had.

Established on the front room sofa, Norman leaned back and stared out the window, down the long lane. Winter was rapidly approaching and soon the snows would come. Winter. He gave a sigh.

"Do you want anything, Dear?" Jenelle asked, laying down her mending and preparing to fetch whatever it was her husband wanted.

Norman shook his head. "No, I was just thinking."

"What about?"

"Winter. Jenelle," he turned towards her with a light in his eyes that hadn't been there for several days, "Orlena has never seen real snow before! Oh, sure, she's seen it in the city where that school is and in Blank City with Grandmother, but city snow is just not the same. I can't wait to watch her enjoy the vast snow covered fields and hills."

"What if she doesn't like it, Norman. It may frighten her."

"What? Frighten her? Nonsense." Norman scoffed at the very idea, for he himself had always loved the snowy landscape of winter and all the enjoyment the cold, white days brought. He even delighted in taking hay out to the cattle in the pastures and took great satisfaction in clearing paths from the house to the barn and bunk house through the glittering piles of snow.

Norman woke from his daydream with a start as Orlena came in from school and the wind caught and slammed the door shut behind her.

"Where is the fire?" Orlena demanded. "There ought to be one. It's freezing outside!"

"Is it really?" Norman reached for his crutches, his eyes alive. "It must have dropped since we were out, Jenelle. Jenelle?" He turned to find his wife's chair empty. "Now where is she?"

"How would I know," Orlena snapped, "I just got home."

A look of concern swept over Norman's face at his sister's tone. "Why don't you sit down for a bit, Sis," he offered, "and tell me about your day."

But Orlena shook her head. "There's nothing to tell

that would interest you, and I have homework to do." With that, Orlena, having hung up her jacket, snatched up her books and hurriedly left the room.

Norman frowned. What was wrong with Orlena? He hadn't heard her that impatient since before his accident. Was she growing sick?

The truth was that Orlena was finding it harder than she had thought it would be to be kind and sweet. Though there hadn't been as much to rouse her temper since Norman had been confined to bed for several weeks and had only been up and about the last week or so, it was still difficult not to give way to the common feelings of selfishness and pride that had been fostered and petted for eight years and which had grown to be such a part of her. There was only one sure way of ridding herself from those constant companions and that one way Orlena refused to acknowledge, so she struggled on in her own way. Often she wondered why it was so hard to be the sweet person she wanted to be.

Up in her own room, Orlena flung her books on her bed and herself into her chair and scowled. The walk home in the chilly wind had only added to the gloominess and self-pity she had felt in school. There she had no particular friends and, though she felt it below her dignity as a granddaughter of Mrs. Marshall Mavrich to make friends with the rough, country children, she did have a little following who were interested in her only because of her rich clothes and her constant talk of money. However, these "friends" didn't always follow her every whim and today had been such a day. Not only that, but Miss Hearter had assigned several pages of arithmetic for her class. This was one subject which Orlena dreaded. For years her examples were worked for her by one of her classmates who could be bribed, but here she was finding it more difficult to get others to do her work, even for money.

When the call came for supper, it found her still seated in her chair. Quickly she started up and hurriedly made herself presentable, knowing that her brother frowned upon lateness at meal times.

Much to her surprise, however, Norman said not a word about her tardiness. Instead he simply asked the blessing and supper was begun.

"Do you have much homework this evening, Orlena?" Jenelle asked pleasantly when the meal was nearly over.

Orlena sniffed. "Yes, I have mountains of it, and I'll never get done. I wish you had let me go away to boarding school, Norman," she pouted. "I know I wouldn't be so overworked. Miss Hearter is just trying to humiliate me because she heard I had been to Madam Viscount's Seminary; she's afraid I'll know more than she does, so she gives me piles of homework so I can't keep up."

"I doubt that," Norman muttered, then in a conversational voice added, "But suppose you bring your homework down here and maybe Jenelle or I can help you. I remember Father helping me several times when I was stuck."

"Father helped you?" Orlena looked up in surprise. She didn't remember her father much at all since she had been only three years old when both her parents had been taken from her in an accident.

Norman nodded, "So, bring your books down and we'll work on them. What is the hardest subject?"

"Arithmetic!" It was said with such vehemence that Jenelle smiled.

"Orlena, you sound like I used to before Norman came along and helped me."

Pausing as she rose from her seat, Orlena stared at her sister-in-law. "Norman helped you?"

Norman chuckled. "I sure did. Did you know that I went to school out here when I lived with Uncle Hiram? I even went to the very same school you're going to now. Of course there was a different teacher then."

For a moment Orlena stood speechless. She hadn't even thought of Norman attending school when he lived with her grandmother's brother "out west." At least not until he went off to college. Just thinking about him and Jenelle attending school together in the same school she was now attending bewildered her. Suddenly Norman didn't seem as old as he had before. Or did he seem twice as old? She couldn't decide.

Her face held such a bewildered and puzzled look that Jenelle laughed and said, "Run along and get your books, Orlena. I'll help Mrs. O'Connor with the dishes tonight." After she had gone slowly upstairs, Jenelle leaned over her husband's shoulder and kissed him. "Be patient with your new student, teacher," she whispered.

Norman returned the kiss without a word, wondering what he had in store for the evening. He soon found out.

When Orlena dumped her books on the table a few minutes later, her brother eyed them in surprise. "It looks like you have more than math here," he remarked with raised eyebrows.

"I told you Miss Hearter has something against me."

Norman bit back a quick reply that rose to his lips. He was determined to be as helpful and patient as he could. "Well—" he winced as he shifted his weight and his injured leg hit the leg of the table. For a moment he just sat still waiting for the pain to subside. Then he continued, "Let's get started on your arithmetic if that is the hardest subject."

The pile of school books was soon in a large, untidy heap on the table as Orlena dug through them to find her slate pencil.

Keeping his voice mild, Norman chided, "Orlena, that is not a good way to treat your books. Stack them carefully and don't tumble them about as though they were wooden blocks. Your pencil has rolled over by Mrs. O'Connor's place."

"Why should it matter to you how I treat my books?" Orlena asked, retrieving her pencil. "They're not yours."

"You should always treat your things with care so that they will last. Put them in a neat stack and then we'll begin. Now," when the other books were stacked though Orlena grumbled about it under her breath, "Copy the first example down on the slate and we'll look it over together."

This was soon done and Norman looked at it. He could see the answer right away, but he carefully walked his sister through the problem until it looked as though she would get the right answer. "Now see if you can finish it," Norman instructed.

Orlena stared a moment at the many figures before her and then dashed off some random numbers.

Shaking his head, Norman erased her answer and said, "That wasn't even close to the right answer."

"I can't do it."

"You didn't even try."

"How do you know?"

"Because if you had even thought for a moment about what you wrote, you would have realized that your answer shouldn't be larger than the number you started with if you are subtracting. Now try it again and this time make the answer correct."

With a scowl Orlena tried again. The answer she scribbled was too small this time and Norman frowned.

CHAPTER 2

A DISTURBING DISCOVERY

Shaking his head he again erased the numbers and said, "All right, let's go over this problem once more; now pay attention." Carefully explaining everything again as he went along, Norman showed Orlena the right answer.

"Oh yes, of course," Orlena nodded.

"See, it wasn't too hard once you gave it your full attention. Copy the next problem down."

This she did and passed her slate to Norman saying, "You can do that one. I'll work on history."

There was a brief moment of silence as Norman stared at his sister in disbelief. She hadn't really said what he thought she had, had she? "Orlena, I'm not doing your work for you."

"Why not?"

"For several reasons. If I did, you wouldn't learn anything. Two, it wouldn't be honest, and three, how would you expect to do a problem in school if you didn't practice here?"

Orlena shrugged. "I'm not called upon to work problems at the blackboard much." She turned to her history book and opened it.

Reaching out, Norman gently pulled the book from his sister's hands and said, "Let's do one subject at a time."

With a resigned sigh, Orlena folded her arms on the table. "Go ahead then. Work the problem, and I'll watch."

But Norman shook his head.

"You surely don't expect me to work all these examples myself, do you?"

"Yes, I do."

Sitting up straight, Orlena stared at her brother. "Norman Mavrich!" she exclaimed. "You said that Father helped you! I think you are just being horrid!" Orlena sniffed. "I thought you loved me."

Norman didn't reply right away but drummed his fingers on the table. His sister needed help, he could see that, but he wasn't sure she would accept the help he had to offer. He wondered what Miss Hearter had to say about Orlena's school work. He'd have to ask her the next chance he got. Meanwhile his sister was waiting. "You are right about Father helping me," he began, "but he never worked my problems for me, and I'm not going to do your work for you. I'll help you understand it and check your work, but it is up to you to do it."

For a moment Orlena stared at her brother. Then, with a burst of tears, she snatched her books and slate. "Then I don't want your help!" she shouted and dashed up the stairs to her room, leaving her brother sitting in stunned silence behind.

"What was that all about?" Jenelle's soft voice caused Norman to turn. "Were you able to help her?"

Wordlessly he shook his head. His sister's reaction was too bewildering to understand. Slowly he reached for his crutches and stood up.

Jenelle watched him somewhat anxiously, for seldom was Norman at a loss for words. "Would you like to go up to bed?"

Norman shook his head. "No, I couldn't sleep now if I tried. What— She— Jenelle, what are we going to do?"

"We're going to go into the front room and talk." Jenelle's voice was calm, and soon they were settled on the sofa and Norman was telling all that had gone on in the dining room.

"I'm not sure what went wrong."

Jenelle was silent a few minutes listening to the ticking of the clock and the rustle of the gold and scarlet leaves outside on the trees. The sun had set and the gas was turned low. It was a favorite way for Mr. and Mrs. Mavrich to enjoy an evening, but tonight they didn't notice the sounds that usually brought so much pleasure. "Perhaps Orlena is just extra tired or is working too hard. I wonder if she's getting enough sleep, or maybe she's growing tired of trying to be good in her own strength."

Norman sighed. "Maybe it's a combination of everything." He sat silently for a moment, his arm about his wife. "Jenelle, do you think that Orlena has had other people do her school assignments for her?"

"Probably."

The calm, matter of fact response wasn't what Norman had hoped for, but he knew it could be the truth. After all, Orlena had money to bribe other students, and being away at boarding school no doubt made it easier to cheat. He wondered what her grades were now and resolved again to have a talk with Miss Hearter as soon as possible.

After more talk and prayer, Mr. and Mrs. Mavrich retired to their room. The rest of the house was dark save for a light which shone out from under Orlena's door.

"What is she still doing up?" Norman whispered. "She should be in bed at this hour."

"I'll make sure she's all right," Jenelle murmured, moving softly to the girl's room. A gentle tap brought some hurried sounds and then Orlena's voice.

"What is it?"

Quietly Jenelle opened the door, and looking in, saw Orlena sitting on her bed with her school books spread around her. She looked slightly flushed and excited. "Are you all right?" Jenelle asked in hushed tones.

"Of course I am." The answer was almost a snap.

"It's late and you should be in bed. Are you nearly through with your homework?"

Orlena snorted and then said quickly, "Almost. I don't see why Miss Hearter gives so much homework. You can go to bed, Jenelle, I'll only be a few more minutes."

"All right. Good-night." And Jenelle closed the door feeling a little doubtful that her sister's homework was nearly done.

When she entered their room, Norman said, "Still working on homework, right?"

Jenelle nodded slowly. "She said she was almost done."

"But you don't think so." It wasn't a question, it was a statement, and Jenelle glanced at Norman's reflection in the mirror as she began pulling the pins from her light hair.

"How did you know I thought that?" she asked.

"By the look on your face, Dear. It's a good thing you never tried to be a spy, for your face would have betrayed you every time."

The room was dark and Jenelle wondered what had awakened her. All was quiet and still. Norman's steady breathing beside her gave proof that whatever it was hadn't disturbed his dreams.

Dong. Dong.

The grandfather clock struck two. Still very puzzled, and finding herself wide awake and a bit chilly, Jenelle slipped from the bed and pulled on her warm wrapper. She would just go and get another blanket from the linen closet. Tiptoeing out to the hall, she was startled to see a light coming from under Orlena's door.

"Surely the child isn't still working on her homework!" Jenelle thought, gliding silently across the hall. There she listened for any sound, but on hearing nothing, she softly opened the door. The schoolbooks were stacked on the table and Orlena was sound asleep in bed. Then why was the light on? Had she simply forgotten to turn it off?

Moving quietly into the room, Jenelle bent over the bed to draw the covers more closely over the sleeping girl. As she did so, her foot bumped something on the floor. Stooping,

Jenelle picked up a small, dime novel and cringed as she read the title. All at once she knew what had been going on. How or where Orlena had gotten the book, Jenelle had no idea, but this might help explain Orlena's behavior and attitude. With a soft sigh, Jenelle turned out the light and slipped from the room.

Lying in bed, Jenelle stared for some time at the light the moon was making on the curtains. Her thoughts were disturbing and several times she was tempted to awaken her husband, but each time she silenced the urge. At last, when sleep seemed to have fled completely, Jenelle slid to her knees beside the bed and prayed, asking for wisdom and courage in dealing with the new problem and pleading earnestly for Orlena to yield herself to Christ.

The clock was striking three-thirty when Jenelle rose from her knees and slipped back into bed. She felt at peace and pulling the covers about her shoulders, she yawned and realized that she had forgotten to get an extra blanket.

When Jenelle next opened her eyes, she saw that Norman was already dressed and was leaning on his crutches beside the bed looking down at her. "So you did decide to wake up after all?" he asked smiling.

Sitting up, Jenelle asked, "What time is it? Is it late? Why didn't you wake me? Is Orlena up? Has Mrs. O'Connor started breakfast? She'll wonder where I am. Do you think it's going to be colder today than it was yesterday?" As she talked, Jenelle was flying about the room getting ready for the day. Suddenly she paused and realized that Norman was sitting in a chair chuckling. "What's so funny? Surely it isn't that late? Norman Mavrich, what is so humorous?" she demanded, stopping in front of him.

"You are, Sweet. How can I answer any of your questions if you don't pause long enough for me to even take a breath?" And Norman chuckled again.

Dropping onto the bed, Jenelle looked at Norman's amused face and then began to laugh herself.

This light, cheerful, not to say merry, mood was a good start to their day and any gloom from the evening's occurrences was dispelled.

It wasn't until after breakfast was over and Orlena had set off for school, claiming that her homework was done, that Jenelle remembered the book she had discovered in Orlena's room. Suddenly her face grew grave and Norman, seeing the change, demanded to know what was wrong.

Lifting troubled eyes to her husband's face, Jenelle said softly, "Come up to our room. I found something in Orlena's room last night."

Puzzled, Norman followed his wife up the stairs and into their room where he sat down and leaned his crutches against the wall. Jenelle hadn't brought anything back from Orlena's room before they went to bed, had she?

Jenelle had opened the closet door and, reaching into the pocket of her dressing gown said, "I think you should see it, but oh, Norman . . ." And clutching the book to her she hurried across the room, dropped onto a footstool and leaning on her husband's knee, burst into tears.

Norman was astonished to say the least. This was not at all like the sweet, merry, lovable wife he knew. What had happened? "Darling, what is it?" he asked again. But Jenelle couldn't talk, and seeing that, and realizing that whatever it was that Jenelle held would shed light on the situation, Norman gently took it from her.

As he examined it, his face grew grave and somewhat stern. He frowned. For some time he remained silent then he coaxed, bending down to kiss her, "Come Dearest, dry your tears, pull up your little rocker and let's talk."

Feeling better for the tears she had shed, and knowing that further tears would be a waste of time, Jenelle pulled up her rocker and waited for Norman to speak.

"When and where did you find this?"

Jenelle related the night's happenings to him and then added, "I don't think she knew it was gone this morning."

"Probably not," was the thoughtful reply. "I wonder

how many more she has?"

Startled, Jenelle searched her husband's face. "More?"

With a tender smile, Norman replied, "You don't think she only has one of these, do you?"

A gust of wind rattled the windowpane and Jenelle shivered, but whether from a draft or the thought of more dime novels, she couldn't have said. "I . . . I never thought of more. Oh Norman, what are we going to do?"

Norman sighed. That was a question he had been pondering. "I wish I could ask her and get a truthful answer about them. But since I can't, I think we should take a look and see if we find any others."

"Norman, if we do find more, what will Orlena say?" The words were a mere whisper.

"Plenty I'm sure."

"I wish we didn't have to look," Jenelle began then paused on hearing footsteps on the stairs. "Perhaps Mrs. O'Connor knows if there are more."

"If she had found any, I'm sure she would have said so. Mrs. O'Connor," Norman called as the housekeeper came down the hall.

Hearing her name, Mrs. O'Connor came to the door. "Did I hear you call me?"

Norman smiled at her. This good woman, housekeeper in his grandmother's large mansion in the city, had, at Norman's request, agreed to come out to Triple Creek Ranch when Jenelle had been ill and had stayed on. Neither Mr. nor Mrs. Mavrich would think of her leaving them, at least not for a long time to come, and Mrs. O'Connor was happy to remain.

"Mrs. O'Connor, have you ever known my sister to read dime novels like this?" And Norman out held the book.

"Aye, to be sure," Mrs. O'Connor sighed. "Tis a sorry thing indeed for a lass like her to be filling her head with such poison. Your grandmother wouldn't let her read them when she knew about them, but tis an easy thing entirely to hide such things in a house so large. Right glad I am to be knowing you've found it out."

"Mrs. O'Connor," Jenelle's anxious voice put in, "did you know she had any of . . . them . . . here?"

"Not for certain, but I had my suspicions and the Good Book says, 'be sure your sins will find you out'."

Moving his injured leg to the stool before him, Norman asked, "Do you think she has more of them?"

Mrs. O'Connor nodded.

"Oh dear." Jenelle's face took on a worried frown. "Mrs. O'Connor, Norman thinks we should see if we can find the rest."

The housekeeper nodded her head in agreement. "To be sure, Orlena wouldn't be telling you if she had more, and it would only bring more trouble if we didn't. Come, I'll go help you. Norman, you remain right there. The doctor said you weren't to overdo it."

"She's right, Norman," Jenelle added. "You rest and we'll see what we can find."

Three quarters of an hour later, Jenelle and Mrs. O'Connor returned with half a dozen dime novels which they had discovered in Orlena's room. Each was as bad as the first, and from the way their covers were torn and curled, it was apparent that they had all been read many times. Under Norman's direction the entire lot were locked securely in a drawer to await a brotherly conference he expected to have with his sister that very evening.

Triple Creek Ranch

CHAPTER 3

CONFRONTATION

It was mid afternoon and a steady north wind had been blowing since morning causing the temperatures to drop. Lloyd, knowing that Mr. Mavrich wouldn't be able to, brought in several armloads of wood for the fireplace in the front room as well as for the kitchen stove.

"Tomorrow'll be warmer again," he remarked, stacking the logs in the wood box in the front room. "Hardrich says it'll probably be summer's last try before winter really sets in. But I'll say it sure doesn't feel like it'll be warm again until spring. Not the way that wind is blowin'." And Lloyd brushed his hands off and stood up.

"Where's Hardrich now?" Norman questioned.

"He was out in the barn when I came in, sir. Think he was checkin' on something he forgot to have me pick up in town yesterday. You want me to give him a message?"

"No, I think I'll just go have a talk with him."

"Norman," Jenelle gasped, "surely you aren't going out there now, are you?"

"Jenelle," Norman chided gently, "I'm not an invalid. It's not going to hurt me to go out to the barn in this weather. I've been out in lots worse."

With a slight sigh, Jenelle smiled. "I know. I just don't want you to get hurt again."

Norman stooped and kissed her. "I'll be careful," he

promised.

Out in the barn, Mr. Hardrich turned in surprise when he heard Norman's voice. "Mavrich, what are you doing out here?"

Norman grinned. "I came out to talk. Hardrich, I think I'll go crazy if Doc doesn't let me get back to work soon! I can stand being an invalid only so long. And now that winter is coming . . ."

Hardrich chuckled. "I reckon there'll be plenty of winter left for you to enjoy when the doctor sets you free."

"I suppose so," Norman sighed dismally, "but I don't want to wait. I never did like waiting for things."

A nicker from the stall nearby caused Norman to turn. "Well, hello Minuet," he said softly, gently rubbing the horse's face. "I've sure missed working with you, but Lloyd couldn't be prouder of you than if you were his own."

"That's for sure," Hardrich put in, moving over beside Triple Creek's boss. "The way he brags on her and how good she's going to be sounds as though he was there when she was born and has worked with her ever since."

Norman smiled. He knew Lloyd Hearter loved a good horse and that Minuet was an exceptionally fine animal.

"Did you really come out here to see me, or the horses, Mavrich?" Hardrich asked, leaning against the stall door.

"I came to talk."

When Norman at last returned to the house, he discovered that Orlena had already returned from school. "It can't be that late," he muttered, pulling his watch from his pocket.

"Mr. Bates was heading to his place and offered Orlena and a few of the others who live out this way a ride home since the wind is so cold," Jenelle explained.

There was no misunderstanding the somewhat anxious look Jenelle gave him and Norman reassured her with a quiet smile. His talk with Hardrich and more especially, the prayer his foreman had offered up before they left the barn, had given him the courage to talk with his sister. "Where's Orlena?"

"She went up to her room saying something about homework."

Thoughtfully the master of Triple Creek Ranch let his wife help him off with his coat and then said, "I guess I'll go up and have the talk with her now."

"Do you want me to be there?" Jenelle asked hesitantly.

Norman shook his head. "No, I don't think there is any need to tell her who found the first book and perhaps it would be better if it were just the two of us. But, Jenelle, pray for me!"

"I will, Dear, I will,"

"And I'll be praying for you too," Mrs. O'Connor said from the kitchen doorway where she stood drying her hands on her apron.

With a brief smile, Norman turned towards the stairs, his crutches thumping on the floor slowly. This was not a task Norman looked forward to, in fact, he dreaded it. His constant prayer as he mounted the stairs was, "Lord, keep my temper!"

The door to Orlena's room wasn't shut all the way when Norman approached having stopped in his room for a moment. "Orlena," he called quietly. "May I come in?"

"I suppose so," was the ungracious reply.

Upon entering, Norman saw his sister seated in her chair while her school books lay where they had fallen when she dumped them on her bed. His eyebrows raised at the sight of the books, but he refrained from speaking. Moving across the room, he pulled out the chair to Orlena's writing desk and sat down. He wasn't sure just how to begin.

Over in her chair, Orlena had been silently watching her brother. Why had he come and what did he want? Norman didn't usually pay her a visit in her room. Perhaps he was going to ask her about her school assignments. It certainly wasn't her fault that he hadn't helped her get them finished on time and that she had been kept in at recess. The memory of the disgrace caused her to scowl. The idea of keeping a Mavrich in simply because her lessons weren't completed, was an insult! Orlena chose to ignore the fact that Miss Hearter had spoken to her several times about her assignments and the punishment was no more than other students received for failing to turn in their assignments.

Norman, wishing to start the conversation calmly, asked, "How was school today, Sis?" He was unprepared for the storm that burst upon him.

"School! It was a perfect disgrace! The school is full of nothing but a bunch of ignorant, backwards children and the teacher is a tyrant. I have been more insulted today than I ever was in my life before and if you love me at all you will see that I am avenged. Why the very name of Mavrich was held in contempt by nearly the entire school! Surely you won't stand for that, Norman. If such treatment is allowed to continue we may as well move right now. It was despicable! Simply and utterly reprehensible!"

Sitting in stunned silence, Norman could only stare at his sister in confusion. What on earth was she talking about? What had happened to the Mavrich name? And what or who was he supposed to avenge? "Orlena, calm down," he broke in at last to say. "I really don't know what you are talking about."

"I am talking about that so called 'school' in town. It's a perfect disgrace and should not be allowed to continue."

"The school shouldn't?"

"Well, I suppose the schoolhouse could remain, but the teacher must be dismissed at once!"

Suddenly light began to dawn in Norman's mind. Something must have happened in school and Orlena had chosen to place all the blame on Lloyd's sister. Not wanting to get involved in an argument over school right then, Norman replied calmly, "I'll look into things at the earliest opportunity."

This was more than Orlena had dreamed she would

hear from her brother and she leaned back in her chair well satisfied. "Just don't take too long," she directed. "There is only so much a person with good breeding such as we have had can stand." Then, after a pause ensued, she asked, "Is that what you came up here for?"

Drawing a deep breath, Norman answered, "No, it wasn't. I wanted to know where you had gotten this," and he drew the dime novel from his pocket.

Orlena gave a slight start at the sight of it and flushed. "What do you mean, where I had gotten it? Where did you find it?"

"It was discovered in your room this morning on the floor beside your bed. Where did you get it?" The question was gently put and Norman waited in silence for an answer.

At first Orlena tried to deny that it was hers, but Norman quietly asked, "Then how did it get in your room?"

"How should I know? Someone must have put it there. Did you ask the others about it?"

"Where did you get the book, Orlena?" Norman wasn't about to be sidetracked into an argument over who had put the book in the room.

"It isn't mine!" Orlena was growing excited.

"I didn't ask if it was yours, I asked where you had gotten it," persisted Norman firmly. "Did you get it the same place you got the other half a dozen novels?"

Orlena caught her breath sharply and looked scared. She knew her grandmother had always been upset whenever she discovered that her granddaughter had "stooped to read such literary rubbish," but Orlena delighted in them. Now her brother had somehow discovered the same kind of books. What would he say and do?

"Orlena, who gave them to you?" By asking a slightly different question, Norman hoped to get an answer from his sister. When none came, he continued, "Come on, Sis, this is serious. This book and others like it are poison. They have ruined many a pure and innocent girl. I won't see that happen to you!" Norman's voice had grown stern and there was a flash in his eyes that Orlena couldn't meet, and her own dropped to the floor.

In a low voice she asked, "What . . . what are you going to do?"

CHAPTER 4

INTO THE FIRE

"I'm going to take them and put them in the fire. That is the only fit place for them." And rising, Norman began to make his way towards the door.

Suddenly Orlena sprang up and dashed to stand in the doorway, stopping him. "Please don't burn them, Norman!" she begged. "You can't!"

"Yes, I can, Orlena, and I'm going to. I will not have such poison on Triple Creek Ranch." The answer was firm and unyielding.

"Norman you can't!" Orlena cried, trying to take the book from his pocket. "You can't burn them, you can't!"

Leaning on his crutches though he was, Norman was able to place a hand over his pocket as he asked, "Why can't I?"

"Be . . . because," the girl stammered.

"If that's all the reason you can give they certainly *shall* go in the fire." Norman quietly put his sister aside and moved out into the hall.

Orlena, becoming desperate, cried out, "But they aren't mine! I was only borrowing them!"

At that, Norman turned. "Who gave them to you?" he demanded.

"Someone." The reply was low, and Orlena scuffed her shoe along the floor, her head down.

Feeling that he was getting somewhere, Norman paused and looked down at the dark hair of his young sister. She was only a child and had never been taught what was truly right. "Who was it?" he asked again, gently this time.

"I . . . I promised not to tell."

"That doesn't matter now; who was it?"

Orlena had never been very worried about keeping promises before, only when they suited her. Now she was afraid that if she told who had lent them to her, her brother would somehow stop her from receiving more. Life would seem terribly dull if she couldn't read her favorite books this winter. But if she didn't tell who gave them to her, Norman would burn them. How was she to explain that to—

Having waited several minutes for an answer to his question and receiving none, Norman turned and moved into his room. He was worried. If he didn't find out who had lent his sister such books, how was he to make sure more of them did not enter his house?

Coming out of his room with the troublesome books in a bag, Norman discovered his sister still standing in the same place he had left her. He couldn't read the expression on her face for her head was still down. Looking at her standing there in the doorway, a feeling of pity, completely new to him, swept over him. She was his sister and she looked so young. "Orlena," Norman said quietly, "are you ready to tell me who gave these books to you?"

She shook her head stubbornly.

With a sigh, Norman said, "Very well," and started slowly down the stairs.

"Norman, where are you going?" demanded Orlena, suddenly roused and frightened.

"To the front room."

"Why?"

By then Norman had reached the bottom of the stairs and had opened the door. Pausing to look up at his sister's anxious face he replied, "I'm going to burn the books."

"No! You can't!" and Orlena dashed down the stairs

after him. "Norman, you can't burn them! They aren't mine!"

Without a word, the master of the Triple Creek continued on.

There was a bright fire in the fireplace thanks to Lloyd, and Norman stopped before it. Jenelle looked up from her rocker where she had been sewing tiny quilt squares.

Before either Jenelle or Norman could speak, Orlena rushed into the room crying, "Norman, don't! You can't burn them. I won't let you!"

Somewhat wearily Norman sank down into his chair, the sack of books in his lap. "Orlena," he began firmly, "if you won't tell me whose books these are, I have no choice but to assume they are yours, and since I will not allow such things on the ranch, they will go in the fire." He looked up at her and waited, wondering if she would tell him who had lent her such unwholesome reading matter; but Orlena was silent.

Reaching into the bag, Norman pulled out a book, the cover of which was curled and torn and without a word tossed it into the midst of the flickering flames. It caught instantly and in a few seconds was nothing but a blaze of blackened flakes.

"No!" shrieked Orlena as Norman tossed the second book after the first. She started forward but, leaning from his chair, her brother caught her arm and pulled her back. "You can't burn them! You can't!" Feelings of helplessness and astonishment were soon swept away by a feeling of anger and Orlena screamed, "Norman Mavrich, don't you dare burn another one of those books! I tell you they aren't mine! I won't let you burn them!" and the child tried to snatch the sack from her brother.

Norman, however, was too quick for her and caught her hands before they could even touch the bag. Though she struggled, Norman didn't relax his grip. "Jenelle," Norman directed over Orlena's cries, "please take the rest of these and put them in the fire."

Knowing that it was for the best, Jenelle did as she was asked.

Norman had shifted his hold on his sister from her hands to her arms after Jenelle had taken the bag, and it wasn't until the last book was only a pile of ashes that he let her go.

For a moment Orlena stared at the fire, not quite believing that all the books were gone. Then, with a cry, she flew up to her own room where she slammed the door, shoved her schoolbooks off her bed and flung herself down to sob wildly. The day had gone from bad to worse. First she had been kept in at recess and now this! Never could she remember such a day. The moaning of the wind in the trees and the slap of a few bare branches against the side of the house only added to the misery she was feeling. For several minutes she sobbed loudly until the many late nights, the struggle over lessons she didn't understand and cared little for, and the emotions of the day had completely worn her out and she slept.

Down in the front room, Norman sat silent and still, his eyes on the dancing flames, his face sober and his shoulders sagging.

For several minutes Jenelle watched him with troubled eyes, wondering what she could say or do. At last she whispered softly, "It's all for the best, Norman."

At that Norman drew a long, deep breath and straightened. "I know. It's just— Oh, Jenelle, I'm afraid it will take Orlena a long time to get over this."

Jenelle didn't reply but, placing her sewing in its basket, rose and moved to perch on the arm of his chair. Her silent sympathy needed no words and when Mrs. O'Connor came in thirty minutes later, both faces were calm.

"Is supper ready, Mrs. O'Connor?" Jenelle asked.

"It is," the older woman replied. "But," she added, "I called Orlena and not one word or sound did I receive. I'd go up, but the soup would stick to the pan if left that long."

"I'll go see—"

"No, Norman," Jenelle shook her head, "I'll see about

Orlena. You've already been up and down those stairs more than you should." Rising quickly Jenelle slipped from the room and up the stairs, her thoughts going back to the first evening Orlena had spent on the ranch and how, as now, she had come up to see what was keeping her. "I wonder if I'll find a haughty princess as I did the first time," Jenelle murmured to herself. "Or if I'll find a frightened and angry child."

Knocking gently, Jenelle waited for an answer, but receiving none, softly opened the door. The room was dim, for the sun had set and no light had been turned on. After turning the lamp up, Jenelle looked at the bed, and her heart melted. The tearstained face on the pillow looked so young and troubled, and even in her sleep the girl cried now and then.

"Oh, the poor child," Mrs. Mavrich breathed with a catch in her throat as she gently removed Orlena's shoes and spread a warm quilt over her. "If only she would come to Christ, she would find all the love and acceptance, yes, and the joy she is looking for." She stooped and gathered the scattered schoolbooks, placing them in a neat stack on the table. Looking once more at the weary face on the pillow, Jenelle suddenly dropped to her knees beside the bed and prayed.

"Father, here is a poor, little, lost lamb. Won't you find her and bring her home? She's out in the dangerous wilderness and the enemy is after her. Oh, Good Shepherd, find this lamb quickly before she gets hurt!"

Then with a soft kiss on the tear-stained face, Jenelle turned down the light and slipped from the room.

Down in the dining room she found her husband and Mrs. O'Connor waiting for her.

"Is she coming?" Norman asked.

Jenelle shook her head. "No, the poor thing is asleep, her face looking so troubled and her pillow was wet with tears . . ." and Jenelle's own face looked distressed.

At breakfast the following morning Orlena didn't

appear, and Mrs. O'Connor announced that she was still sleeping.

"Perhaps we should let her stay home from school today, Norman," Jenelle suggested. "At least for the morning. If she cried herself to sleep last evening, as I'm sure she did, she probably will wake up with a sick headache."

"I suppose one time wouldn't hurt," Norman began, "but I don't want her to get in the habit of crying herself sick just so she can skip school the next day."

Thus it was that when Orlena awoke the sun was already well up. For a moment she lay in bed staring at the window. "Isn't today a school day?" she thought. She was sure it was. Then why hadn't anyone awakened her? Quickly she sat up, but at the sudden movement her head began to pound and she lay back on her pillow. The events of the evening rushed over her and a feeling of self pity swept into her heart. She had tried to be good over and over, but everyone had conspired against her.

It was nearly noon when Orlena made her way downstairs, her face pale and her hair hanging loose about her face instead of being pinned up in the correct fourteen curls she always insisted on having.

Jenelle, coming in just then from the front room where Norman had been established earlier that morning with instructions to rest, greeted her sister with a smile. "Good morning, Orlena, is your headache any better?"

"How did you know I had a headache?" Orlena asked.

"You looked as though you did when you were sleeping. Is it any better?"

Orlena shrugged. "A little, I suppose."

"Something to eat might help. Let me bring you some toast, and would you rather have a glass of fresh milk or some tea?"

With another shrug, Orlena replied, "I don't care," before sitting down at the table and leaning her head in her hand.

The food did help, but Orlena still felt listless and tired.

She didn't ask why she had been allowed to remain home from school. She hoped it was because Norman wanted to settle the matter of her disgrace before she went back.

When the noon meal was served, Orlena was still sitting at the table and her brother greeted her kindly. "Perhaps we can work on your homework assignments this afternoon, Sis," he told her.

Still feeling sorry for herself, Orlena only nodded. It might be better to take what help she could get and finish her homework and not risk the disgrace of being kept in from recess a second time.

"Jenelle," Norman said, leaning back in his chair after eating his fill, "the weather is so beautiful today, let's go outside for a bit."

It did look pleasant, for the sun was shining in a clear blue sky and the cold winter wind which had blown yesterday had changed into a gentle, caressing breeze. The trees had dropped the rest of their leaves of crimson and gold, russet and brown, and they now lay like a thick carpet upon the ground. All morning long, Jenelle had yearned to be out, but her housework and her husband had kept her inside. Now here was a chance. Her eyes sparkled and eagerly she agreed but then added with concern, "You won't overdo it, will you, Norman? Perhaps we should stay inside."

"Nonsense! You're just being fussy, Sweet," Norman teased with a grin. "It would take more than you and Mrs. O'Connor to keep me inside this afternoon," and he grinned rather boyishly at the housekeeper.

The air was perfect, not so cold that a heavy coat was required, yet a light wrap was just right. "It's on days like this that I wish I could mount Captain and ride off as far as I wanted across the fields. I'd give him his head as I used to do with Sugarboy, my first horse, and away we'd fly." Norman moved his crutches and gazed out across the fields.

"If you were well, I'd mount Minuet and go along with you," Jenelle dreamed, squeezing Norman's strong arm.

"We'd spend the entire afternoon together out on the range and only come back when we were hungry."

"Not even then," Norman promised. "I'd shoot a rabbit or a pheasant and we'd roast it over a fire for our supper."

Jenelle gave a sigh of pleasure. "It does sound fun, Dear. Maybe come spring—"

She was interrupted by the sound of a rapidly approaching horse. The Mavriches both turned to see Lloyd dashing up on Spitfire. The horse was breathing hard as Lloyd reined up quickly at sight of his boss.

"What is it, Hearter?" Mr. Mavrich demanded as Lloyd sprang off his horse looking excited.

"It's Gregory. There's been some sort of a fight, and the sheriff's arrested him and some others, and he's in jail now."

CHAPTER 5

BUSINESS IN TOWN

"He says it wasn't his fault and asked me to come tell you. Sheriff says he can't let him out till he talks with you and some others."

"What?" Norman gasped. "Saddle Captain, and I'll ride back now."

"No, Norman!" Jenelle exclaimed. "You can't ride a horse yet!"

"Hitch up the carriage," Norman called to Alden and Scott who had come from the barn.

"Norman!"

"What's this all about?" Triple Creek's foreman hurried over from a corral. "What do you need a carriage for?"

"I'm going to town. Greg's in jail, and I don't mean to let him stay there if he's not guilty."

"Why don't you let me go," Hardrich offered, seeing the way Jenelle clung to her husband's arm.

Stubbornly Norman shook his head. "Nope. I'm going. Lloyd can drive in with me. I'll have a talk with the sheriff and Greg and then I'll stop by Doc French's and see him. After that I'll make a stop at the schoolhouse and have a talk with Connie. I just can't stay here doing nothing." Norman talked quickly and both his foreman and his wife could see that he was determined to go.

"Then be careful," Jenelle begged, as Alden drove up

with the carriage.

"I will. Lloyd!"

The young hand passed the reins of his horse to Scott who he knew would take good care of Spitfire and then climbed into the carriage. "Don't worry, Mrs. Mavrich, I'll bring him back to you safe and sound."

Jenelle waved her hand and then turned to the foreman with a wry smile. "I wondered how long he'd be able to put up with his confinement."

Hardrich nodded. "But he's sure likely to catch it from Doc when he sees him. Now what was that about Gregory?"

"I don't really know," Jenelle said. "Lloyd said there'd been a fight, but—" she shrugged, leaving her sentence unfinished.

"Well, I reckon we'll find out what happened once those two return." After a few more minutes of conversation, Jenelle returned to the house and Hardrich to the barn.

On the way to town, Norman pressed Lloyd for more information about the fight and Gregory being arrested, but Lloyd couldn't tell him much more than he had already told him.

Upon arriving in Rough Rock, Lloyd drove straight to the sheriff's office and Norman, with some difficulty, climbed down. "I don't know how long I'll be, Hearter. You can come along with me if you want or you can spend the time as you please. Just don't you land in jail."

"I reckon I'll come along with you. At least until you reach the doctor's. That should keep us both out of trouble," Lloyd replied, tying up the horse and grinning at his boss.

Norman laughed.

"Well, Norman Mavrich!" Sheriff Hughes exclaimed, rising from behind his desk to come forward with an outstretched hand and a warm smile on his face. "I was planning on paying you a visit later on this evening. I certainly wasn't expecting you to come all the way in here. Sit down. How's the leg? Mrs. Mavrich doing all right?

"She's fine, Sheriff. Leg's doin' well, though all this inaction is enough to drive me crazy. Now what's this I hear about you holding Zach Gregory in jail?" Norman had taken the offered seat while the sheriff perched on the corner of his desk and Lloyd leaned against the wall.

"Well, it started, as best as I can figure," the sheriff began, "as a brawl in the saloon. But it ended up out in the street and several bystanders got mixed up. Gregory was one of them. My deputy wanted to break things up quickly so he just hauled the lot of them in here to let me sort it out." And Sheriff Hughes shook his head.

"If Gregory wasn't involved except by accident, then why're you still holding him?"

"Safety. You see, in defending himself he, well, he broke Con Blomberg's nose."

"Oh."

The sheriff nodded. "Now you see why he's still here?"

Norman nodded. Con Blomberg was a wealthy, no-good resident of Rough Rock who had more money than he knew how to handle. He also possessed a violent temper and a bragging mouth. The saloon was his favorite place to visit and he was dangerous to most people who crossed him, with the exception of the sheriff and Norman Mavrich. After a couple of run-ins with Mr. Mavrich, in which he had gotten the worst of things, Con Blomberg stayed away from him and the Triple Creek Ranch hands. At least until that morning.

"I was hoping," the sheriff continued. "that you could take Gregory back to Triple Creek, for a while at least. I know you let him go because winter is coming on, but if he stays around here, the only safe place for him is going to be in that jail cell where he is right now."

Norman nodded thoughtfully. If he had the full use of his leg and was as robust as he had been before the accident, he would have confronted Con that afternoon. However, that was not the case, and Norman agreed to take Gregory back to the ranch when he left town. "Let me have a few words with him now, Sheriff," he said, rising. "I don't think he'll mind waiting then until I'm ready to leave."

"Sure thing."

Gregory was delighted to see his boss again and agreed to wait until he and Lloyd were ready to return to the ranch. He wasn't anxious to have a run in with Blomberg or anyone in his pay.

Outside once more, Lloyd asked, "Where to now? School's not out yet."

"I reckon I'll just pay Dr. French a call. It might save him the trouble of calling on us."

"In that case," Lloyd grinned, "I'd best be gettin' over to see Ma. Just don't tell Doc I'm the one who brought you."

"Only that it was your fault I'm here." Norman laughed as his young hand groaned. "Once I'm through there, if school isn't out yet, I'll stop by your place."

Lloyd nodded and turned towards his home in town while Norman limped his way across the street.

As Hardrich had predicted, Dr. French gave Norman a mild tongue lashing for disobeying his orders. "You ranchers are all so used to giving orders," he growled, "you've forgotten how to take them. Humph!" And Dr. French shook his head. After that the two men had a pleasant conversation and the doctor promised Norman that his leg was coming along wonderfully and so were his ribs and it wouldn't be much longer before he'd let him get back to his work around the ranch. The truth was that Dr. French knew just how hard it was for these men to give up everything they loved doing and lie around playing the invalid instead.

When Norman left the doctor's office, it was nearly time for school to let out and he decided to pay Mrs. Hearter a call after he had talked with the school teacher.

Arriving at the school, he paused and watched the children dash from the door, racing for home. The shouts and calls of "Let's stop and buy some candy!" "Hurry up, Susan." "Pa said it's going to snow soon." and "Wait for me,

Ted!" brought to Norman's mind his own school days and how he had raced back to the ranch eager to ride his horse or help with the chores. For several minutes after the last child had disappeared down the road, he continued standing, lost in thought. At last he made his way up the steps and into the schoolhouse where he discovered Lloyd's sister sitting at her desk no doubt grading papers.

"Miss Hearter," Norman said, taking off his hat and hobbling up the aisle.

Connie Hearter looked up quickly. "Mr. Mavrich! What brings you here? Is Orlena sick? I missed her in school today. How's Jenelle?"

"Jenelle's fine. Orlena wasn't feeling well this morning and we let her stay home. I did come to talk to you about her though, if you have time."

"Why, of course I have time." Miss Hearter rose from her chair as Norman, dropping his hat on top of a student's desk, sank down behind it. Taking a seat across the aisle, Miss Hearter said, "I was thinking of driving out to Triple Creek to talk with you and Jenelle, but you have saved me the trouble."

Norman gave a slight smile. "Glad to know I can still be of help even with these things," and he glanced at his crutches. "But getting right to the point, Miss Hearter, Orlena has problems."

Miss Hearter nodded but said nothing.

Nervously Norman fingered his hat for a moment, picked it up and then set it back down. "I'm not even sure where to begin," he began at last. "She told me some rather mixed up story last evening about being 'insulted' and the 'Mavrich name held in contempt'." He sighed and looked with a puzzled expression at the teacher.

With a slight smile, Miss Hearter explained. "I kept her in at recess yesterday because her lessons were not done. I've talked with her a few times about them, but when nothing seemed to work, I had to do something. I imagine that was the problem."

Norman nodded. "More than likely. I wonder," he

added dryly, "what she would say if she knew that I'd been kept in during recess and after school because I had ridden my horse instead of doing my lessons." He paused. "Now that that's cleared up, what are her grades like?"

Miss Hearter's face sobered. "Not very good, I'm afraid. She tells me she was in a very advanced school before coming here, but I'm finding out that some of the very basic lessons in arithmetic seem to never have been learned."

"They probably weren't."

"She does all right in history, and in reading she is exceptional, but," Miss Hearter sighed, "in anything else she is, well, . . ."

Norman rubbed the back of his neck thoughtfully. "I can see how much of this lack of knowledge came about. I don't know for sure, of course, but I am pretty confident that she paid some of her schoolmates to either do her math for her or at least to let her copy the answers. And it probably wasn't only mathematics either."

"I wondered if that might be the case."

"Are there any students here who might be tempted to cheat or help someone else cheat for money?" Norman asked quietly.

"I wish I could say no," Miss Hearter began, "but there are a few who seem to be fairly devoted to your sister. None of them are exceptional students, but all have more knowledge of mathematics than Orlena does. I haven't been able to find out anything definite yet, but don't think my eyes aren't open."

"Thanks." And Norman sighed, staring at the blackboard. Slowly his fingers began to tap the top of the desk. The sound of a crow out in the trees behind the schoolhouse was loudly harsh and insistent. At last he spoke again. "Besides her school work, how is my sister doing?"

"She has been doing better. At least she was doing better, but the last few weeks she seems to have returned to her earlier— well . . ." the teacher paused and hesitated.

"Please, Miss Hearter," Norman said, "don't try to

spare my feelings. I know what my sister is like. And I know she acts like a brat sometimes."

Nodding, Miss Hearter continued, "Her work has sadly slacked off, she doesn't pay much attention in class and her homework isn't done. At first I thought it was a reaction to your injury, but now . . ."

In a quiet voice, Norman said, "Miss Hearter, it appears that Orlena has been getting dime novels from someone in town. She won't say who it is, but she denied being the owner of them. She's obviously been staying up late to read or reading when she should have been working on her homework. I think that's the cause, or at least part of the cause, of her current problems. As far as I know the only ones she knows in town are her schoolmates."

The school teacher's face wore a look of concern. "Oh, Mr. Mavrich, that would explain why she's behaving the way she is. And she won't tell you where she got them?"

Norman shook his head. "I was hoping you might have some idea."

Slowly shaking her head, Miss Hearter replied, "I can't think of a single parent who would let their child read dime novels, and no one else in class has turned in poor work. But," she added, "I will be watching now and if I see or hear anything, I will let you know."

"Thank you, Miss Hearter," Norman sighed. "Frankly it hasn't been easy with Orlena on the ranch, but we keep praying."

Softly Connie Hearter said, "I'm praying too, and I know Mother never lets a day pass without praying for each of you. Lloyd never gossips about the ranch, but from the few things he's said, and knowing Orlena as I do in school, it isn't hard to see at least a glimmer of what you are going through."

"We appreciate your prayers, Miss Hearter, and those of your mother." There was deep feeling in Norman Mavrich's words. "Thank you for talking with me. Now I know how Orlena stands in her studies." Norman stood up.

"And I assure you we'll be working with her this winter. I know she is capable of doing fine work if she wants to."

"I'm afraid that's where the trouble lies, Mr. Mavrich," Miss Hearter had also risen and held out her hand. "It does help though that she has a brother as dedicated to doing the right thing as you are. Thank you for stopping by."

Norman shook the offered hand, picked up his hat and headed towards the door, his crutches moving slowly down the aisle of the schoolhouse. The talk with Orlena's teacher, though it hadn't solved everything, had shed new light on his sister's schoolwork, and the fact that prayers were going up from the Hearter home for Orlena gave him renewed faith.

T

CHAPTER 6

PREDICAMENTS

Making his way slowly towards the Hearter home, Norman became aware that his leg was beginning to ache and he felt more tired than if he had spent the day in the fields. "Humph," he said to himself, "Norman Mavrich, no more breaking any bones, it makes you too soft and lazy."

The Hearter home was a small, grey house set back from the street. A large tree grew in the front and the ground was covered with leaves which crunched delightfully under Norman's slow tread. When he reached the front door, it was opened for him by a young girl of about Orlena's age, though her sweet and innocent face was a marked contrast to Orlena's.

"Good afternoon, Mr. Mavrich," the child greeted him brightly. "Ma said you were to come right in. Lloyd went to bring the carriage around because he said you shouldn't walk any more."

Norman smiled. "Thank you, Charity." Just the thought of walking across town to the sheriff's office again had made him feel exhausted. Before he had been injured he would have thought nothing of walking through town or even out to the ranch, but now— He sighed.

"Norman Mavrich, come right in and sit down. You shouldn't be doing so much walking with that injured leg." The voice belonged to a frail looking woman seated in a rocking chair near a bright fire.

Gratefully Norman sank into a chair. "Hello Mrs. Hearter. It does feel good to sit down and relax. I never dreamed that a trip to town could make me so tired."

Mrs. Hearter shook her head. "I'm surprised the doctor let you come in."

At that Norman gave a rather sheepish grin. "He didn't, and I got a tongue lashing for doing it. But some things you just have to do yourself."

Mrs. Hearter clicked her tongue and then said, "Have a cup of tea while you wait for Lloyd. It would never do for you to catch a cold."

When Lloyd and Gregory arrived in the carriage some ten minutes later, Norman was feeling more rested and ready for the drive back to the ranch. Gratefully he thanked his hostess for her hospitality, bid Charity and Connie, who had just come home from school, farewell, and with Lloyd's assistance, climbed into the carriage.

The men in the carriage were quiet as Lloyd headed the horse towards the main street of Rough Rock. The sun was well down in the west, and Norman knew it would be dusk when they arrived home. He hoped Jenelle wouldn't start to worry.

"I expect we'll have snow before long," Gregory remarked from the back seat. Though he had been christened Zacheriah Gregory, he was nearly always called Greg by those who knew him. And the name seemed to suit him.

A sudden shout startled the men, and instinctively Lloyd drew rein to see what it was about. A showily dressed man had moved away from the saloon and now took a staggering step towards the carriage. "There he is," the man shouted, pointing a finger at Greg. "He's sa man that broke my nose! I'll jus' see how he likes havin' no nose s'tall." His words were a bit slurred and it was obvious that he had been drinking. Reaching down, he began to draw his gun when a sharp voice, cracking like a whip stopped him.

"Don't touch that gun, Con Blomberg, or you'll have me to reckon with."

Blinking, the man turned to stare somewhat stupidly at the men in the front seat of the carriage. "Whoshe dat?" He asked of the men who had stopped and were gathering about to watch the showdown.

"That's Norman Mavrich, Blomberg. I reckon you'd better leave well enough alone," one man told him, taking his arm and trying to lead him back into the saloon. "You can't fight him, especially not when you're half drunk."

"You let go my arm," Blomberg snarled. "I ain't 'fraid a Norman Mavrish an' I ain't drunk. Jesh took a bit a shomething fer the pain. Jesh fer the pain." Then he repeated, "I ain't 'fraid a Norman Mavrish."

"Well, he ought to be," muttered one of the bystanders to another who nodded in agreement.

The half drunk man took a step closer and moved his hand towards his gun belt. Without a word Norman held out his hand to Lloyd. The young hand simply drew his six-shooter and handed it to him. Normally Norman Mavrich would have had his own gun strapped to his side, but he had left the ranch in such a hurry that he hadn't even thought of it.

"Blomberg," Norman's sharp voice again arrested the man. "Don't touch that gun."

In the silence that followed his words, everyone heard the soft click of the six-shooter in Mr. Mavrich's hand. "If you try to draw that gun, Blomberg, I'll have no choice but to shoot it out of your hand."

The crowd drew farther away from the man addressed. They knew Mr. Mavrich was a dead shot, always hitting what he aimed for, but even so it was better to be on the safe side.

"Das not gintlemanly of ya, Mis'er Mavrish," Blomberg whined.

"It's not very gentlemanly of you to threaten the company I'm with," Norman retorted quietly.

For a moment Blomberg seemed to consider the matter

and then he said, "I won't draw my gun, Mis'er Mavrish, if ya tell that shnake ta climb down an' take wash comin' to 'im."

"I'll do nothing of the kind and you had best watch how you talk about my friends! Now move on."

"I ain't taken no ordersh from you, Mis'er Mavrish," Blomberg growled. "Dish here ish my town an' if I wan'a shoot shomeone's nose, I'll jesh do it."

"Not in my town you won't!" a new voice said sternly, and Sheriff Hughes crossed the street and grasped Blomberg's arm. "Perhaps a night in jail will calm you down." Then, turning to the occupants of the carrige, he said, "Drive on, Hearter."

Lloyd slapped the reins, and the horse started off at a brisk trot for home.

It wasn't until they were well out of the town that anyone spoke.

"I'm mighty glad you were there tonight, Mr. Mavrich," Greg sighed. "Things might have gotten ugly back there. Thanks."

"Don't mention it," Norman replied quietly. "Here's your gun, Hearter, thanks for the use of it."

Taking the gun, Lloyd slipped it back in its holster without a word.

The sun had set and the dusk was quickly deepening into night. The air, which had been so pleasant before, grew cold and Norman shivered. His leg ached and he was tired. Pulling his hat lower, he folded his arms trying to stay warm.

"Here, sir," Lloyd said, "put this on," and he placed his own jacket on his boss's lap.

Norman looked up in surprise. He hadn't realized that anyone had noticed that he was cold. He shook his head. "I'm all right. Put it back on, Hearter or you'll be sick."

Stubbornly Lloyd shook his head. "No sir. I promised Mrs. Mavrich I'd bring you back safe and sound and I mean to do it."

Norman was about to protest, but Greg interrupted. "You can put your jacket on, Hearter, I have my coat here. It might be a better fit for the boss anyway." And a warm coat was put about Norman's shoulders.

But it was only after Lloyd had put his own jacket back on and Greg had insisted that he was already wearing a jacket, that Norman reluctantly agreed to wear the coat. He hated to admit that he was so worn out by the trip to town that the cool night air was too cold for him.

At last the lights of the ranch house were seen below them and they were driving up the lane. The carriage had hardly stopped before Jenelle, Mrs. O'Connor, Hardrich and the other hands were gathered about, all asking what had taken them so long and was everyone all right.

There was no chance to answer, for Norman was helped down and hustled as quickly as his crutches would go, into the warm house where Jenelle bustled about to make him comfortable and Mrs. O'Connor brought him his dinner which she had kept hot for him.

The room was only dimly lit as Jenelle spread another quilt over the bed. The cold night air spoke of winter, and now and then a gust of wind would whistle around the house. Norman lay looking up from his pillow at his wife and smiled. "Jenelle," he said softly, "stop worrying. I'll be all right after a good sleep."

Sitting down on the bed beside him, her hair loose about her shoulders, Jenelle laid a tender hand caressingly against her husband's face. "I'll try not to," she whispered. "But you were so late in coming, I almost sent Hardrich and the men to find you."

Silently Norman slipped his hand up from under the blankets and clasping the small hand, kissed the fingers. "We would have been here sooner, but I had a slight exchange of words with Blomberg." And Norman told of the meeting.

When the tale was told, Jenelle shook her head. "I sometimes wonder what will happen with that man if he keeps on the way he is. Now, Dear, you should sleep." She tried to withdraw her hand, but Norman held it fast.

"I'm not tired any longer," he told her. "And I want to talk." He started to sit up, but Jenelle quickly pushed him back down.

"If you must talk, do it right there," she said, smiling. "I'd like to hear about the day."

A light dusting of snow lay on the ground in the morning and the sky was overcast. Now and then a few more flakes would drift down, but Hardrich predicted it would clear up before noon and the snow would stop. Orlena pouted about having to go in to school with snow on the ground, but no one listened to her complaints and at the regular time she set off, wrapped up warmly, for she wasn't yet used to the cold of the open west.

Mr. and Mrs. Mavrich had settled themselves in the front room before a bright, warm fire when the sound of a deep voice and then the tramp of boots on the floor in the dining room was heard. "We're in here, Hardrich," Norman called. "Come and pull up a chair. The fire's just right."

Triple Creek's foreman entered the room and pulling up a chair, grinned.

"What's up?" Norman asked, eyeing Jim Hardrich with puzzled eyes.

"Well, it just occurred to me that you might not have heard the news."

"What news is that, Mr. Hardrich?" Jenelle asked, looking up from the sock she was knitting.

"Just the news about Greg."

"Hardrich, what are you talking about? I just rode back from town yesterday with Greg and he didn't say much of anything. What news is there about him that we haven't heard?"

"He's taking a wife."

"What?" Both Mr. and Mrs. Mavrich turned to the speaker in astonishment.

"How come he didn't say anything about it yesterday?" Norman demanded. "He had time enough in the carriage."

"That's where it gets amusing, Mavrich. You see it's like this," And Hardrich leaned back in his chair and prepared to tell the story.

"Yesterday in town, Hearter had picked up the mail for the ranch and had it in his saddlebag when he heard the news about Greg. All thoughts of it completely left his mind until this morning when he brought it in. There was a letter for Greg from this girl saying she'd marry him come spring."

"Spring!" Norman stared at his foreman as though he had lost his mind. "Who is this girl? When did he ever meet her? Where's he planning on living? Did he plan on telling me this or was it to be a surprise?"

Chuckling, Hardrich replied, "Well, fact is Greg was a bit nervous about talking to you and asked me to do it for him. Nope, he's never met the girl, but apparently his brother's wife back east knows her from the old country. She's just arrived in America."

"Where is she from?" Jenelle asked.

Hardrich scratched his head. "I don't rightly recall, but you could ask Greg, he'll know, I think. He's been writing to his brother, and his brother has been sending his letters to the girl when his wife writes to her. He's sure she'll fit right in with ranch life—"

"Hang on a minute there, Hardrich," Norman interrupted. "Is Greg planning on buying a ranch of his own or of heading off somewhere else to start one?"

With another grin and twinkling eyes, the foreman shook his head. "That's just it, he's hoping you'll hire him on this spring as you have the last few years."

"Of course I'd like to hire him. He's a good hand, but where on earth is he planning on living?"

When Hardrich didn't reply, Norman groaned. "Hardrich, don't tell me he's wanting to stay here? What about his wife?"

"Dear," Jenelle suggested, "why couldn't they stay in that old cabin back beyond Crystal Creek? I know it needs some repairs, but—"

"Huh uh," Norman shook his head. "Sorry, Jenelle, I can't do it." Before she could ask or say anything else, he added, "Do you know what would happen if I let one hand live on the ranch with his wife? The rest of them would all find wives and expect to live here too. We'd end up with more children than cattle after a few years and there'd be so many houses that the cattle wouldn't have any place to graze."

CHAPTER 7

FIRST SNOW

"But—"

"Jenelle, would you want cattle grazing in your front yard?"

She shook her head.

"Would you want them looking in your window to see what you were fixing for supper? Or bawling because you were eating their herd friend?"

Again she shook her head, and this time a smile twitched at the corners of her mouth.

"Would you want cattle following you everywhere, eating your wash, chewing up your flowers, crowding your doorway?"

Jenelle laughed. "You win."

"Hardrich, suppose you tell him that if he can find a place in town to live, and is willing to come out to the ranch each day, I'll keep him on. Or I can hire him as I do Thompkins and a few of the others who have families; I'll hire them when I need help with the round-ups."

Hardrich grinned. "Those were my thoughts exactly. Now," he asked, changing the subject, "What are your plans for next week?"

When Orlena came home after school, Norman greeted her. "How was school today?"

"All right," Orlena shrugged.

"Once you finish your chores suppose you bring your books to the table and I'll help you."

For a moment Orlena looked at her brother in surprise. "Why?" she asked.

Norman's eyebrows raised. "Why? Because I thought if your homework was done before supper then we could do something afterwards without worrying about school assignments."

"I don't have to do any homework today," Orlena told him. "There are two days before another day of school comes."

"True, but it's always pleasant to have it done and out of the way, don't you think?"

Orlena shrugged. The truth was that she had never experienced the freedom of having her schoolwork finished ahead of when it was due. Always before she had waited until the last minute to work on it and often had to finish the last of it before she left for school. She wondered what they would do after supper. They had never done anything before, why were they going to do so now?

Norman was watching his sister's face and he could tell that she was hesitating. He decided that a little explanation might be necessary so he said, "Since it is winter, and it gets dark so early, we often tell stories, sing or play games after supper."

"Just you, Jenelle and me?"

"And Mrs. O'Connor. We couldn't leave her out. And sometimes the men will join us." He saw a look of disgust start to creep over her face, so he added quickly, "Have you ever heard Jim Hardrich tell a story?"

Orlena shook her head.

"Or heard Alden play the fiddle?" When Orlena shook her head again, Norman exclaimed, "Well! Let's try to get your homework done. But first run up and change and take care of the chickens. I'll have your books ready when you come back."

Norman's enthusiasm had been catching and much to her own surprise, Orlena found herself quickly changing into a dress Jenelle had sewn for her. She discovered that it was much warmer than the city dress she had worn to school. Rapidly she hung up her school dress and then raced down the stairs, flung her coat on and dashed outside.

Jenelle and Mrs. O'Connor, not having heard Norman's conversation with Orlena, turned in astonishment as the child flew past them. What had happened? Quickly Jenelle, with a spoon in one hand and a bowl in the other, stepped into the dining room. Norman was whistling as he arranged Orlena's schoolbooks on the end of the table.

"Norman, what has happened?"

"To what?"

"To Orlena."

Norman only glanced up briefly. "Oh, that. We've decided to work on her homework before supper in hopes that it will be done soon enough for us to enjoy the evening together since it is winter."

"Well!" was all Jenelle said as she blinked at her husband's bent head and listened to his whistle. He hadn't whistled since his accident. Perhaps this winter wasn't going to be as hard as she had thought it might. Her thoughts might have changed had she heard Norman twenty minutes later.

"Orlena, we've got to do something about your arithmetic. Either you haven't learned what you should have learned years ago, or you just aren't paying attention."

With a pretty pout, Orlena replied, "I've tried, but everything is a muddle with numbers; they're always changing things."

"No they aren't. But we'll start at the beginning and won't move on until you've gotten it."

This wasn't exactly what Orlena had in mind when her brother had said he was going to help her, but there wasn't much she could do about it, for she was discovering that it was difficult to get him to change his mind. The only thing she could hope for was that he would get busy with things on the ranch and forget all about it, but his next sentence didn't sound promising.

"It'll be a winter project. The days when you can't go to school, we'll work on any subjects you're behind on, but especially on math."

"When won't I be going to school?" Orlena asked.

"When the snow's too deep. There could be several weeks at a time that school is closed. At least there will be days."

Orlena turned and stared at her brother. She couldn't imagine that much snow. "Norman, it doesn't really snow that much—" She hesitated. "Does it?"

"Sometimes." Norman's reply was easy. He'd always delighted in the days when the snow had kept him from attending school. "Now, let's get on with the books."

It was a lovely evening. A blazing fire in the fireplace glowed, casting bright lights and strange shadows about the room. Mrs. O'Connor and Mrs. Mavrich were each settled in rockers with knitting or sewing, Norman, his injured leg resting on a stool, was relaxing in his favorite chair before the fire mending a bridle, while Orlena, curled up on the sofa, watched the flames and wondered at the novelty of it all.

"This reminds me of one night when I was thirteen," Norman began. "It was the year I spent out here when our parents were abroad for Father's business, and I loved nearly every minute of it. The evening was cold and crisp just like tonight, and Uncle Hiram was sitting in his chair before the fire snoozing. I was supposed to be doing my homework, but I had recently been given a new bridle for Sugarboy, he was my horse then, and I was longing to try it out." He paused to grin at the remembrance before continuing. "I should have known better, but seeing Uncle asleep and knowing that the hands would be in the bunkhouse, the temptation was too much and I slipped out. The stars were so bright, and there was an almost full moon. I hurried to the barn, saddled my horse and led him out past the corrals before I mounted him.

That ride was one I never forgot. Sugarboy seemed to enjoy the ride as much as I did and it was late when I arrived back at the barn. There wasn't any light on in the house and I figured Uncle had gone to bed thinking I had too. Quietly I took care of my horse and then, as I was closing his stall door, a lantern was lit and a voice said, 'Decided to come back, did you?'

"I must have jumped ten inches, I was that scared. For a moment I couldn't talk. But when I realized that it was just Mr. Hardrich and not my uncle, I began to breathe easier and even replied, 'Yep, it was a lovely night for a ride. I'll see you in the morning, Mr. Hardrich.' But he placed a hand on my arm and asked where I was going.

"I told him off to bed, but he said he wanted to see Uncle and would go with me. I knew then that there was no hope of getting into the house and up to bed without Uncle knowing." Norman shook his head, his hands falling idle in his lap and staring into the flames remembering.

"What happened, Norman?" Orlena begged when her brother had remained silent for nearly a full minute.

"What happened? Oh," and Norman finished his story. "Well, Hardrich, still with his hand on my arm, walked into the house and called, "Hiram! Here's your boy.' I had expected Uncle to be up in his room, but to my surprise, he came from this front room. 'So he came back by himself, did he?' Hardrich nodded. 'And did he take care of his horse?' Hardrich nodded again. For a moment Uncle just stood looking at me, and I began to squirm.

"I knew then that Uncle had known about my ride even before Hardrich had brought me in. Perhaps he had stood by the window and watched me take the horse from the barn and leave.

"After what seemed like hours to me, Uncle Hiram said, 'Thanks, Hardrich, I'll deal with him.' Hardrich left the house and I was alone with my uncle.

"It was another minute before he spoke directly to me. 'How was the ride, Norm?' I began to become hopeful as I told him how pleasant it was and how well Sugarboy had behaved. Perhaps Uncle would just let me go to bed with a mild reproof. However, my hopes were dashed. 'A ride in the night alone like that can be mighty dangerous, Norm. Even if it weren't, you still disobeyed. Haven't I told you you weren't to ride your horse until your lessons were done?' I nodded. He had told me, but I had chosen not to listen. I knew then that he had seen my lessons sitting in the front room unfinished.

"I tried a feeble protest, 'But it was such a lovely night, and I couldn't ask you because you were asleep and . . .' but somehow I couldn't finish. 'Had you asked me, I might have gone with you,' Uncle said, unbuckling his belt. I knew my time had come."

Norman shook his head again. "I couldn't sit comfortably on a saddle all of the following day, but never again did I try riding off without permission."

"Tut, tut!" Mrs. O'Connor exclaimed. "'Tis a wonder you weren't killed entirely, riding off by yourself like that."

Norman chuckled. "Don't be too hard on me Mrs. O'Connor; I got what I deserved when I returned, and any time I stepped out of line, for that matter."

Looking up from her sewing, Jenelle smiled and said softly, "I think you turned out just fine."

A swift, tender look passed between Triple Creek's master and his wife.

T

There was no new snow on Saturday, but it was bitterly cold. Orlena wandered about the house for a time, wondering what to do, until her brother insisted they spend an hour working on her arithmetic. This wasn't exactly what Orlena had in mind for spending a cold winter morning, but she saw she had no choice and, deciding it was better than doing nothing, complied reluctantly.

It was a difficult hour for both Norman and Orlena, for the latter was not interested in learning the things she had never learned and saw no reason why she should learn them now. As for Norman, it was trying for him to have to go over and over the simplest of math facts and still have the answer be wrong. At the end of the hour, after Orlena had left the dining room, Norman stared across at the wall a moment and muttered, "It's a good thing I never had to teach for a living."

T

Large, white snowflakes were falling silently on Monday morning when Norman looked out of the window. "The first real snowfall of the year, Jenelle," he exclaimed quietly, but with excitement. "If it weren't for this leg, I'd be out seeing how Minuet does in the snow or saddling up Captain to take Orlena to school."

Moving across the room to stand beside him, Jenelle brushed back the curtain and peered out. It was still dark, but the falling flakes brought a bit of lightness to the world outdoors. "It looks so pretty. Do you think it will snow all day?"

"Probably not all day," Norman replied. "But at least most of the morning."

"Do you think Orlena will be all right walking to school this morning?"

Norman looked down in surprise. "Why wouldn't she be? You walked to school in more snow than this."

Laughing softly, Jenelle looked up, "Yes I did, but Norman, don't forget that I was raised in this country and Orlena wasn't. I also had my three brothers with me. Orlena doesn't have anyone."

"I hadn't thought of that." A slight frown crossed Norman's face, and he tapped his fingers on his crutches. "Well, I could have one of the hands drive her in this morning, but she'd have to walk home alone. If I'd taken the time to teach her how to ride earlier this fall, she could just ride to school. There's always room at the livery for the children's horses."

"Well, it's too late to teach her to ride this morning," Jenelle said, hearing Mrs. O'Connor's steps in the hall. "I must go down and help prepare breakfast. Are you going to come down now too?"

Breakfast wasn't quite over when the sound of a horse approaching broke the silent winter morning. "Now who could that be at this time?" And Norman rose slowly, grabbed his crutches and made his way to the door. "Why Carmond, what brings you out this time of morning?"

Jenelle looked up at the sound of their neighbor's name. Had something happened at the Running C?

Mr. Carmond's words set her fears to rest. "I thought I'd take Flo and Jenny to school this morning and it occurred to me that your sister might like a ride as well. It'll be a cold walk in this weather with it snowing and all. I was out for a morning ride and decided to stop by before I headed back home. Should I pick her up?"

"Carmond, that would sure take a load off my mind if you would," those in the dining room heard Norman answer. "If I weren't on these crutches, I'd take her in myself, but as it is, I'd be much obliged."

"Then I'll be by a little later. Hope that leg gets well real soon." And Mr. Carmond moved away from the door.

"Thanks again," Norman called after him before shutting the door against the cold, wet snow which fell.

Coming back into the dining room, Norman smiled. "There you are, Sis, a ride to school."

CHAPTER 8

RESTLESS WAITING

"You won't have to leave as early now and you won't be out in the cold as long."

Finishing her breakfast in silence, Orlena wasn't sure if she was pleased at the prospect of a ride to school or not. She knew Flo and Jenny; Flo was one of the oldest girls in school and Jenny was a year or two younger than Orlena. Both girls were quiet and sweet and Orlena had never had much to do with either of them. But the prospect of walking to school in the snow was even less appealing; therefore, she shrugged, swallowed the last of her milk and disappeared back upstairs to finish getting ready.

Mrs. O'Connor, seeing that everyone was through eating, began to clear away the dishes but pausing at the window, looked out over the fields which were turning white in the falling snow. "Ah, tis much like the old country," she sighed. "It's often I've felt a wee bit homesick for the sight of the fresh snow without the dirt of the cities or smoke from the factories to mar its beauty."

Norman couldn't agree more. "There's nothing quite like it, is there?" He moved slowly across the room to stand beside the older woman and gaze out over the vast expanse of Triple Creek Ranch.

Pausing before she carried the last of the dishes to the kitchen, Jenelle smiled at the two standing so still in silent enjoyment of the thousands of snowflakes drifting down from the white clouds above. She also enjoyed the snow and the pleasures that winter brought, her favorite being the long days she could spend with her husband, but there was work to do and, leaving Norman and Mrs. O'Connor to enjoy the view from the window, she set about washing the dishes.

It wasn't until she heard the sound of a wagon driving up the lane and Orlena coming down the stairs and departing that Mrs. O'Connor suddenly awoke from her dreams of long ago and realized that Jenelle would be nearly through with the dishes.

"Jenelle, why didn't you call me?" Mrs. O'Connor scolded, hurrying into the kitchen and seeing Jenelle wiping the last of the dishes.

"Why should I?" Jenelle smiled back. "I don't mind washing the dishes, and you seemed so far away, I hated to disturb you."

"Aye, I was far away," agreed Mrs. O'Connor. "Far away in another time and another country entirely."

The morning passed by slowly for Norman who moved restlessly from window to window, watching the snow come down and the ground slowly change from drab brown to a frosty white, as the flakes found their way down between the tall grasses of the fields. Often Jenelle would stop her work and beg her husband to sit and rest, but Norman was too restless to remain still for long and soon he would be up again, the sound of his crutches on the floor giving added proof that he longed to be out and about again.

When the morning was nearly over, Norman saw a horseman turning in to their lane and wondered who could be stopping by. "Jenelle," he called.

Quickly Jenelle hurried into the room, her hands covered with flour from making bread. "Yes?"

Norman held the curtain back and pointed to the horseman as he approached. "Isn't that the sheriff?"

"It looks like it. But what would Sheriff Hughes be

doing all the way out here?"

Norman shrugged and turned from the window. "I reckon he'll tell us." And he hobbled over to open the front door while Jenelle hurried back to her bread.

"Come in, Sheriff," Norman invited. "What brings you out here?"

Sheriff Hughes stepped inside and took off his hat. "Can't stay long, Mavrich. I'm heading back from Silver Spur. Bittner thinks he saw a prowler 'round his barn last night and sent one of his hands in to town this morning to fetch me. Any tracks that might have been there were covered up, but Bittner's still sure about what he saw."

"Well," Norman began. "I haven't been out much, but I'll check with Hardrich and the hands and tell them to keep an eye out. Wouldn't hurt to be cautious."

"That's what I figured," the sheriff said nodding. "I also thought I'd mention that it might not be a bad idea if Greg stayed away from Rough Rock, for a couple weeks at least. Blomberg is still mighty upset about his nose and, well, you know what his temper is like."

Norman nodded. "I'll tell him. Greg's not one to back away from a fight though."

"That's what I mean," Sheriff Hughes said. "It's just that he might not win and we'd have trouble."

"Well, I'll see what I can do. Thanks for stopping by, Sheriff."

"Sure thing, Mavrich. And let me know if anyone here sees anything suspicious."

"Will do."

The Sheriff put his hat back on and stepped outside. Mounting his horse, he glanced back and lifted a hand in farewell before riding off.

Norman watched him go and then, shutting the door, hobbled into the kitchen. The smell of bread baking was tantalizing and he sniffed the air. "A fellow can grow mighty hungry when he smells fresh bread baking," he hinted with a grin.

Jenelle looked up and laughed. "I don't think you want it quite yet, Dear."

"Your dinner will be on the table in ten minutes," Mrs. O'Connor told him. "You won't be starving in that amount of time."

Silently, leaning against the doorframe, Norman stood and watched the preparations for the noon meal. After he ate he'd go talk with the men.

It wasn't easy to get to the bunkhouse with the snow on the ground, but Norman reveled in the challenge and wouldn't hear of his wife going with him. He put his coat on with little difficulty and grabbed his hat. "Who knows how long I'll be there," he told her. "It's been a while since I've been out to the bunkhouse and I want to talk to the men. Don't fret over me, Sweetheart. It's stopped snowing and before long I'll be out in the snow all day long." He flashed her a grin and added, "You'll soon have to give up your job of looking after me, for as soon as Doc gives me leave, I'm tossing these crutches and will start giving orders around here again." He put a finger on her nose as he spoke.

Pushing his hand away with a merry laugh, Jenelle pulled her husband's face down and kissed him.

It was harder moving through the snow with crutches than he had thought, but it wasn't deep and after a short time Norman arrived at the door of the bunkhouse. Before he had a chance to reach for the latch, the door was opened from inside and Hardrich stood before him smiling. "Enjoyed yourself, didn't you?" he asked.

"Yep."

There was a general commotion as the men, realizing that their boss had arrived, left whatever they were doing to crowd around and greet him. At last Norman was allowed to move farther into the room, having been divested of his coat and hat, to sit down in a straight backed chair.

"If any of you start fussing over me," Norman threatened with a scowl, but with merry eyes, "I'll wash your face with snow as soon as I'm done with these things," and he dropped his crutches on the floor with a crash. Then he grinned. "I get enough fussing at the house."

The men exchanged smiles. It was good to see Mr. Mavrich in such a mood. Everyone settled back down to whatever they had been doing and listened as Norman told them about the sheriff's visit and Bittner's suspicions.

"Did any of you men notice anything unusual this morning?" he asked, glancing about the room. "Any strange footprints or things out of place?"

Everyone shook his head.

"Well, keep your eyes open and let me know if you notice anything. Sheriff said Bittner was convinced he'd had a prowler and if he did, he may still be hanging around."

"I wouldn't think he'd be hanging around too long, Mavrich," Alden commented. "Not with the snow and cold."

"I agree. It's one thing to spend the day out in the snow, it's another to spend the night. Well, keep a sharp eye on things anyway."

Hardrich nodded. "We'll do that."

A silence fell over the group, a silence of comradeship, where no one felt the need to talk but just enjoyed being together.

For several minutes Norman sat, watching his men as they mended bridles, polished saddles, cleaned boots and whittled. There wasn't much work to do these early days of winter, but once the snows grew deep, feed would have to be taken out to the pastures for the cattle. Thinking of the work, Norman was reminded of what else the sheriff had said and he turned to find Greg.

"Oh, Greg, the sheriff talked to me about you this morning."

Gregory looked up from the piece of wood he had been whittling. "About me, sir?"

Norman nodded. "Yep. It seems as though Blomberg is still rather upset about his nose and the sheriff thinks it would be a good idea if you stayed out of Rough Rock for some weeks. At least if you value your skin."

"Why that——" Greg began.

"Now, hold on, Greg," Norman admonished firmly. "Don't you go losing your temper just because Blomberg has. Just listen to my idea. I'd like to keep you on at Triple Creek this winter, but it's not worth while with the small amount of work we have to do. So why don't you take the train back east for the winter."

Every man in the room raised his head and looked, first at Norman and then at Greg. They'd never expected to hear Mr. Mavrich tell someone to skip town just because of some hot head. Surely, if they all went into town together, they could deal with Blomberg.

On seeing the looks exchanged, Norman couldn't help letting a slight smile creep over his face. He knew what the men were thinking.

"I hear you have a girl back east who said she'd marry you come spring."

Greg turned rather red and muttered, "Yes sir."

"Well, why don't you, as I was saying, take the train back east, spend the winter with your brother's family and get to know this girl. You could even marry her back there so your brother and his family could attend. Then, in the spring, bring your bride back to Rough Rock and settle down. You could live in town or buy yourself a small piece of land and start your own ranch. By then Blomberg should have forgotten his nose and moved on to other things. What do you say?"

For several minutes Greg sat in silence, fiddling with the wood and knife in his hands and shuffling his foot uneasily. At last he looked up and said with a sigh, "All right. I'll go. I'm not wantin' to go back east, but I reckon you're right 'bout Blomberg. He'd keep remembering if I were around all winter. No," he sat up and squared his shoulders, "I reckon I'll take the next train east. I'd like to meet my girl anyway."

"By the way, where is she from?" Norman leaned

forward to ask.

"She's from England," Greg replied with pride. "An English girl to wed an American cowhand."

"Ought to make an interesting couple," St. John remarked. "Have you told her you don't drink tea?"

A general laugh went up from the hands and Greg good-naturedly heaved a boot at the big ranch cook. Not one of the cowhands drank tea and Lloyd seemed to be the only one who knew how to make it. The silence was broken and a general flow of conversation sprang up.

For the time, Norman forgot about his crutches and was again one of his men, swapping stories and talking about the winter days which lay ahead and the work that would need to be done.

"Think we'll get more snow soon, Hardrich?" Scott asked.

Hardrich glanced out the window and up at the sky. "Not today." He shrugged. "We could, but I don't think we'll get much more in the next few days."

The talk drifted from the snow to other things as the minutes slipped by and soon turned to hours.

Suddenly the door of the bunkhouse was opened and Dr. French stepped in. The men turned in surprise. When had he arrived?

Upon seeing Norman, Dr. French said, "I told your wife you'd be sitting out here talking. She was growing worried."

"Why would she be worried about me? I told her where I was going."

"Humph," Dr. French grunted, taking his coat off. "I suppose you don't realize that you've been out here nearly all afternoon. I brought your sister home from school."

"What?" And Norman started up in astonishment.

"Now you stay right there," the doctor ordered. "Let's see how that leg is getting on. I know I checked it on Thursday, but I hear you've been using it. Tramping through the snow, indeed!" he muttered. "You ranch men are all alike.

You never learn." As he spoke he pulled up a chair before Norman. Dr. French wasn't really as gruff and sour as he sounded and the men knew it. His bedside manners were those of a tender but firm father while his understanding of the problems of his patients had earned him a much respected place in the hearts of those in Rough Rock and the surrounding ranches.

After a careful examination of Norman's leg and ribs, the doctor grunted and, without a word, turned to Scott. The men sat in silence, watching and waiting.

CHAPTER 9

BACK IN THE SADDLE

It wasn't until Dr. French had risen and was pulling on his coat that he spoke. "Well, Scott, I'll let you get on a horse again if you can stick this time. Just go easy on the lifting. If you feel pain in your ribs, get some help. Not that you will," he added, knowing full well that ranch hands rarely ask for assistance. "But at least I've discharged my duties."

Scott grinned. At last he was free to do his usual work. He could hardly wait to get on a horse again.

Then, turning to Norman Mavrich, who sat silent with his grey eyes fixed on the doctor's face, he said, "By the time your leg's in shape to ride again, your ribs will be just fine. I'm going to let you start putting a little weight on that leg. Mind I said a little!" He spoke hastily, for Norman's face had lit up. "Overdo it and I'll send you back to your bed."

Norman promised to be careful.

"Humph," was the answer. "They all say they'll be careful." He slapped his hat on his head and picked up his bag. "And you stay off of the horses."

"Thanks, Doc. I will. For now." Norman couldn't resist adding as the doctor turned towards the door.

At his words, Dr. French wheeled and ordered, "You'd best come with me to the house before your wife comes out looking for you."

When they were outside, Norman said seriously, "Tell

65

me, Doc. how much longer do you think I'll be stuck with these things?" And he shoved the crutches into the snow before him.

"I'm thinking not much more than a week. Unless something happens, such as a slip in the snow and a re-breaking of the leg, I promise you'll be off before Thanksgiving."

Norman sighed with relief. "Thanks Doctor, for everything." He held out a hand as the doctor reached his buggy. "And thanks for bringing Orlena home."

The days passed by. Greg was driven to the station by Hardrich, where he bought his ticket and was soon steaming away towards the east where his girl was awaiting him. Norman exercised his leg and waited with what patience he could for the doctor's permission to mount a horse and get rid of his crutches, while Jenelle and Mrs. O'Connor spent the days taking care of the house and sewing. Both ladies enjoyed the long winter evenings before the fire, busy with their handwork while they talked or Norman told stories. Resenting her brother's insistence that her homework be completed at the dining room table and that he check her work, Orlena had fallen back into some of her old ways. True, she hadn't let her temper get complete control of her as it had before Norman's accident, but it often made the evenings unpleasant until her work was finished.

Winter had settled down over the ranches and a continuous blanket of snow lay everywhere. There was still tall grass to be seen, and the men of the ranch had yet to take feed out to the cattle. Though they had watched, the prowler which Bittner had seen on the Silver Spur hadn't been sighted on the Triple Creek, and most of the hands believed it had either been a joke or Bittner's imagination.

"I've checked around each of the buildings in the

mornings," St. John told Hardrich, "and I haven't seen any sign of Bittner's prowler."

Hardrich shrugged. "And you might not. It was most likely just someone passing through that thought the Silver Spur's barn a pleasant place to spend the night."

T

At last the day Norman had been waiting for arrived, and Dr. French gave him leave to return to his work if he took things easy the first few days. No sooner had the doctor driven away in his sleigh over the snow covered roads, than Norman exclaimed, "I'm going out to saddle up Captain. I'll just ride to town and pick up the mail." He walked quickly across the room, limping slightly.

Jenelle, laughing at his excitement, equally delighted to know that her husband was well again, caught his arm and said, "You aren't going anywhere yet. It's time to eat."

Halting, Norman paused to consider. "All right," he agreed with a laugh. "I'll stay and eat before I go in to town. Do you want to come along?"

"Oh, Norman, I'd love to, but . . ."

Norman smiled. "We'll ride another time. Maybe I'll just take Hearter and let him stay in town for the night. He hasn't been to town for a while and who knows when a big snow storm will hit."

"Just so you don't get stuck in town," Jenelle smiled sweetly.

"No fear of that. Captain would find his way back to his stall even if I couldn't see. But I might wait for Orlena."

Mrs. O'Connor stepped into the dining room with a steaming dish and set it on the table. The smell was tantalizing and no one needed any urging to sit down and partake.

"Orlena, where are my books?"

Orlena turned, clutching her school books against her. She had pulled on her coat and was about to leave the school house for her walk home when Elvira's low words stopped her. "I don't have them," she whispered, glancing around to see if any of the other students were within hearing.

"Where are they?"

"My brother found them."

"You didn't tell him whose they were, did you?"

Orlena gave Elvira a look of superior disgust. "Of course I didn't."

"Well," persisted her schoolmate, "where are they?"

Hesitating for a moment until a few students had brushed past them, Orlena leaned forward to say, "He burned them."

"He what!" Elvira exclaimed, forgetting in her excitement to use caution.

"Girls, is there something wrong?" Miss Hearter's voice, calm and quiet, startled the two girls who looked up quickly.

"No, ma'am," Elvira said quickly. "We were just talking."

Miss Hearter looked for a moment at the girls' faces before saying quietly, "Well, it's time you were both on your way home."

"Yes, Miss Hearter," Elvira said quickly, grabbing Orlena's arm and pulling her out the door with her.

"Come on," she urged, "walk with me for a ways."

Somewhat reluctantly, Orlena let herself be pulled off the main road. She didn't really like Elvira, but she had let her copy her work now and then when Miss Hearter wasn't watching.

With a merry whistle, Norman rode into Rough Rock. He felt wonderful and his horse, Captain, seemed to feel the same way, for he pranced along as though it were a spring morning instead of a winter afternoon. Drawing up before the schoolhouse, Norman dismounted and, dropping the reins, made his way to the door.

Miss Hearter looked up as he entered. "Mr. Mavrich! What brings you by? You're not on crutches!"

"Nope. Doc. finally said I could ride again, so Captain and I came out to pick up the mail and I thought I'd take Orlena home too. Did she already leave? I didn't see her."

Miss Hearter's face, which had looked so pleased at Norman's news, clouded. "Yes, she's already gone, though I'm surprised that you didn't see her. She left with Elvira Ledford."

Norman frowned. "Elvira Ledford," he repeated, "of the Bar X?"

Miss Hearter nodded. "I'm not sure what they were talking about in whispers by the door, but I know Elvira pulled Orlena along with her."

"Hmm." Norman was thoughtful. "Thank you, Miss Hearter." He turned to go. "You'll find Lloyd at the house. I've giving him the rest of the day off. He can come back to the ranch tomorrow."

With a smile of thanks, Miss Hearter returned to the papers on her desk as Norman hurried back out to his horse.

Riding slowly along down the street, Norman headed in the direction of the Bar X ranch while he looked everywhere for his sister. What was she doing with Elvira?

Orlena was growing angry. "I already told you that I can't get the books back, and I have no way of getting you new ones," she snapped.

"Well, you'll have to do something," replied Elvira with equal heat. "I lent those books to you with the understanding that you'd take care of them and not let anyone find out. Now it turns out that you couldn't do either. You have to do something," she repeated.

"You should be glad I didn't tell Norman who gave them to me," retorted Orlena. "I could have, you know." And she tossed her head defiantly.

"If you do, I'll never let you copy my work again!"

threatened Elvira. Then she seemed to have an idea. "You're rich enough, you can just give me the money for them." And the girl held out her hand.

"I don't have the money with me," Orlena said pertly.

"Then get it and give it to me before school tomorrow or I won't let you copy."

Orlena wasn't sure just how she was to get it, for she had no more spending money. She had used it all to bribe her classmates to let her copy their work. The rest of her money from Grandmother was put away and inaccessible to her. Perhaps Norman would give her a little more. She wouldn't have to tell him what it was for.

Before anything more could be said, Orlena heard her name called and, turning, saw her brother riding up on his horse.

"You're on a horse," she gasped.

Norman grinned. "Sure am. I thought you might like a ride back to the ranch. Oh, good afternoon, Elvira," and Norman, as though noticing his sister's companion for the first time, touched his hat to her.

"Good afternoon, Mr. Mavrich," Elvira replied sweetly. "I'll see you tomorrow, Orlena," she added, before turning away.

There was something in her tone and the meaningful look she gave Orlena that puzzled Norman. He didn't know Elvira Ledford very well, but knew her father as a strict and determined rancher. Always before he had thought of Elvira as quiet and sweet, but now he wasn't so sure. There seemed to be a hidden meaning in her good-bye to Orlena, but what was it?

As these thoughts moved through his mind, Norman hadn't been idle. "Hand me your books, Orlena. I'll tuck them in my coat pocket." Pulling his foot from the stirrup he added, "Now put your foot in here and swing up behind me. Captain won't mind carrying us both."

Orlena, having handed her books up, hesitated. She had never ridden a horse before in her life and the thought of it rather frightened her. "I . . . I . . . I think I'll walk," she stammered.

Raising his eyebrows, Norman looked down at his sister in surprise. Why would she rather walk? Suddenly it dawned on him. "Orlena," he asked quietly, "have you ever ridden a horse before?"

Wordlessly she shook her head, her eyes fixed on the ground.

"That's partially my fault. I should have made sure you learned how to ride this fall. I just got caught up in the round-up and then the accident and I neglected it. But come on. All you have to do this time is sit behind me and hold on."

"I . . . I can't get up there," Orlena said.

"Sure you can. There's nothing to it really. It's easier than climbing a tree."

"I've never climbed a tree in my life, Norman Mavrich!"

Norman drew a deep breath. He had forgotten for the moment that his sister was a city girl who was brought up to "be a lady." Somehow he had to get her on the horse. He tried again. "All right. Put your left foot in here, and I'll help you up."

Orlena looked actually terrified as Captain, not liking to stand around in the cold for so long, moved restlessly.

Norman calmed him quickly and then reached a decision. Dismounting, he lifted his sister and set her in the saddle before she could protest. Then he quickly swung himself up behind her, clicked to his horse and they were off.

As they started forward, Orlena gave a slight scream and grabbed the saddle horn, the only thing she saw to hang on to. Not one word could Norman get her to say and, had he seen her face, he would have understood why. Orlena was actually speechless with fright. Even the security of her brother's arms around her didn't lesson the terror she felt. Still fresh in her memory was a trip she had taken with Grandmother and some friends to a horse race. It was a large one, but there had been an accident and Orlena had watched in horror as a horse stumbled and fell, knocking two other horses down and badly injuring his rider. Added to that was Norman's more recent accident on Captain. Was it any wonder that she was terrified to be on the back of a horse?

Triple Creek Ranch

CHAPTER 10

DETECTIVE WORK

Since Orlena wouldn't talk, Norman began again to wonder what Elvira Ledford and his sister had been talking about. And was there something in the look that had been flashed from the girl's eyes? Perhaps he was reading too much into it. But Miss Hearter had sounded almost concerned when she had mentioned them leaving the schoolhouse together. Norman's brows drew together as he puzzled over the situation, going over Elvira's words and Miss Hearter's until they began to grow confused in his mind.

At last, putting it all aside, he began to whistle. Captain, on hearing the sound, pricked up his ears and quickened his pace.

Orlena gave a gasp and Norman could feel her shaking. "Are you cold, Sis?" he asked.

Orlena shook her head.

"Then what's wrong?"

"What . . . what if he falls?" The tones were full of fright and Norman, sensing it, hastened to ease her fears.

"Captain's a steady horse," he reassured. "He won't fall. The snow isn't slick."

"But he fell with you."

"That was different. The ground was a slippery, muddy mess and there were cattle everywhere pushing and shoving us. I think I tried to turn him too fast and he lost his footing.

Anyone could have slipped that night, even if you weren't on a horse. Don't let my accident keep you from enjoying a ride on horseback, Sis. You can't live on a ranch and not know how to ride. Come spring, I'll teach you how. Before you know it you'll be riding as well as Jenelle or one of the hands."

Orlena wasn't so sure she wanted to learn to ride a horse, but she didn't say anything.

By the time they had reached the ranch, Orlena had begun to relax in the saddle and Norman smiled to himself. "I just need to give her some time and she'll get used to a lot of things," he thought, reining Captain up before the house.

Swinging down, he assisted his sister to dismount and handed her the schoolbooks he had put in his pocket. "Tell Jenelle I'll be along as soon as I take care of Captain," he told her. "I won't be long."

It was late in the evening, supper was over and the small family had enjoyed an hour of storytelling around the fire in the front room while a howling wind whistled around the chimney like a wild beast. Mrs. O'Connor had retired and Jenelle had gone upstairs to get a few extra blankets from the linen closet, for the night was promising to be bitterly cold.

Hesitating in the doorway, Orlena, who had risen to follow the ladies, turned. Somehow she had to get money for Elvira before school tomorrow. Perhaps Norman wouldn't ask questions. He had been in a good mood all evening. But what if he asked her why she wanted money, what would she say?

"Orlena?" Norman had noticed her standing in the doorway. "Is there something wrong? Did you want something?"

Putting on a pleading look, Orlena nodded and said, "I want a bit of spending money."

"What for?"

It was the question Orlena had been puzzling over how

to answer. "Why, just because. Didn't you like to have spending money when you were my age?"

Norman laughed. "Not really. What do you want to buy?"

Orlena shrugged.

"You ought to know what you are going to do with the money before you have it, Sis," Norman remarked looking at her quietly. "Why this sudden wish for money?"

A small cloud appeared on Orlena's face as she answered, "Some of the children at school don't think I have any money and I wanted to show them I was rich."

"Not a very worthy use of the article in question," Norman remarked dryly. There was something strange about his sister asking for money. She had never asked for any before and she had been with them several months. "What happened to the money you brought with you from Grandmother's?" Norman had remembered that his sister's purse had held an amount of spending money much larger than he thought wise for a child of her age, yet he had refrained from saying anything, for the places Orlena could spend the money at Rough Rock were very few. "I thought what you had would last you a year."

"A year? The money from Grandmother?" Orlena looked shocked. "Why, that is long gone! That was only enough for a month and I've been here four months." Her voice changed to a whine. "I haven't asked for money before. Please," she begged. "I only want a little."

For a moment Norman sat in silence. What was behind all this? There was something he was sure. "Orlena, come over here and sit down." He motioned to Jenelle's rocker which was across the fire from him.

Reluctantly, with slow steps, Orlena crossed the room and sat down. Perhaps it would have been better to ask about money when Jenelle was around.

When she was seated, Norman began. "Let's get a few things straight here. It is true that you haven't asked for money before, but I can't let you have more unless I know how you are spending it. What did you spend the money you had on?"

"Norman," Orlena sniffed. "How am I supposed to remember all the little things I've spent money on? Money was made to spend, and so I spent it."

"Didn't your schoolmates know you had money before?"

"Yes, but—" Stopping short, Orlena realized her reason for wanting money had been spoiled by a slip of the tongue.

Norman nodded. "I didn't think it was to impress your classmates. What is the real reason?"

There was no answer right away and Orlena's eyes were fixed on her shoes. She couldn't tell Norman the real reason. Or could she? What would happen if she did tell him about Elvira? She knew she dare not bring any more dime novels into the house, and why should Elvira be able to read them if she couldn't? But if Elvira found out that she had told, she'd never let her copy again. It was a struggle, and Orlena didn't know what to do.

After waiting several minutes in vain for his sister to answer him, Norman asked, "What were you going to use the money for?"

"I was going to . . . give some away."

Had Orlena been looking at her brother, she would have seen his eyebrows rise suddenly and a look of skeptical disbelief cross his face. "Huh," he said, "I hardly think so." Then with a shrewdness often noticed and commented on by the townsfolk and other ranchers, he asked, "Does Elvira Ledford have anything to do with this?"

Silence.

"Orlena, look at me." Slowly the girl raised her eyes to her brother's face. "Is Elvira the one who lent you those dime novels?"

The flush on Orlena's cheeks turned to scarlet and she dropped her eyes without a word. How did he know?

She didn't have to speak, however, for Norman had

read her face quite accurately. He sighed. "Orlena, is Elvira expecting you to pay her for the books I destroyed?"

The nod was the very faintest of movements and almost imperceptible.

"Does she expect it by school tomorrow?"

Another nod. How did Norman know all of this? Had he been close enough to hear the whole time she and Elvira had been talking?

A stronger gust of wind than usual rattled the windows and Norman glanced across the room. "I don't think you need worry about school tomorrow. If it doesn't stop snowing tonight we'll have at least a foot of snow on the ground, if not more. I don't imagine you'll be going to school for a few days. But it is late, and you should be in bed."

"But you'll give me the money before I have to go back, won't you?" Orlena pleaded.

Resolutely, Norman shook his head. "No, I can't do that, Orlena. It would have been much easier if you had told me who it was at the beginning, but we can't change things that have already taken place. Don't worry about it now; I'll take care of it."

That was just want Orlena didn't want. "But Norman," she protested, "you can't let anyone know that you know! I promised I wouldn't tell!"

"You didn't."

"But if anything happens she'll think I did and then she'll never let me—" she broke off abruptly in confusion.

"She'll never let you, what?" Norman's voice was firm and grave.

"Be friends," Orlena finished lamely, not meeting her brother's keen grey eyes which were looking so searchingly at her.

A log snapped in the fireplace shooting a shower of sparks up the chimney. Norman wasn't sure he should push his sister for more information just then, though he wished he knew what she had been going to say. He sighed again. "It's time you were in bed, Orlena. We may have a foot of snow in the morning and you may be staying home from school, but that doesn't mean morning won't come early." Orlena had risen slowly. "Good-night, Sis," Norman said quietly. "Sleep well, and don't worry about Elvira. I'll take care of things."

Without a word other than a low "good-night" Orlena slowly, dejectedly made her way out of the room and up the stairs, passing Jenelle in the dining room with only a nod. Things hadn't worked out the way she had hoped they would. What would Elvira say when she found out that Norman knew who had lent her the books he had burned? What if she told him about letting her copy answers during school? What would he do? Greatly upset and agitated, Orlena quickly prepared for bed and crawled under the covers, not realizing that Jenelle had thoughtfully spread another blanket over her bed.

"Norman?"

Norman looked up from the fire he had been staring into. Jenelle stood in the doorway. "Is everything all right?" When he didn't answer right away, Jenelle slipped into the room and went to him. "What has happened with you and Orlena? She looked a little upset and scared when she went up to her room."

With a sober face, Norman reached up and pulled his wife to his lap. "I found out that Elvira Ledford was the one who lent those books to Orlena and now she's trying to get Orlena to pay for them."

Jenelle leaned her head against the broad shoulders of her husband, delighting in the fact that he was well and strong once more. Aloud she said, "Tell me what happened."

When he had finished, she murmured quietly, "Poor Elvira, but I'm not surprised."

Norman looked down in wonder. "You're not?" he asked. "Why?"

"Well," Jenelle sought for the right words to express the feelings and impressions she had received of the Ledford family. "I know Mr. Ledford is a good rancher, you've said so yourself. But I've always felt that he was too concerned about the outward show of things and not what was really important, the heart. He's gruff and stern with Elvira and I'm sure, though I can't tell you why I am, that Elvira is hurting inside. She is a perfect little angel around her elders, but there have been a few times when I've seen her with her friends and all her sweet, winning ways have vanished. In a way, she and Orlena are a lot alike. They are both hurting and confused. Each thinks that being able to slip into another world of excitement and romance will make them happy, but it doesn't. They each need Jesus Christ to make them whole."

Norman's arms tightened about his wife. How well she seemed to know others. Somehow her words made the pain that had been in his heart, lessen. "Thank you, Sweet," he whispered. "That has helped. Let's pray for Orlena right now and then head up to bed."

Norman had been right, the morning came early. Mrs. O'Connor and Jenelle were busy finishing breakfast preparations in the kitchen while Norman, enjoying his freedom from care for his leg, tramped about the dining room waiting. All at once a cry was heard from upstairs and Norman paused to listen.

"Norman!"

Quickly he hurried to the stairs, with Jenelle and Mrs. O'Connor not far behind. There he was met by a white faced, thoroughly frightened child who clung to him and cried, "It's gone! It's gone! They're both gone! Norman, what happened?"

For a moment Norman was stunned. He thought Orlena wasn't awake yet. "Calm down, Sis," he soothed, holding her tightly in his arms but looking bewilderingly at Jenelle. "Everything is going to be all right. Nothing happened that I can't take care of. Hush now."

Gradually Orlena became calmer, but she raised her tearstained face and repeated, "But, Norman, they're gone.

Both of them! What happened?"

Completely puzzled and realizing that Orlena was indeed awake, Norman asked, "What are gone? Orlena, stop crying and tell me what is gone."

"The . . . the barn and the . . . the bunkhouse. I can usually see them from my window but they're gone."

Sudden light dawned on Norman and he smiled. Looking over at Jenelle, who had remained nearby when Mrs. O'Connor returned to the kitchen, he said to her, "I'll explain things if you need to finish breakfast." Then he smiled down at his sister. "There's nothing to be frightened of, Orlena. We're having a heavy snowstorm and there's so much snow blowing around that the barn and the bunkhouse can't be seen. But don't worry, they're still there. I expect the snow will let up in a little while and then you'll be able to see both buildings."

"Are you sure?" she asked. Never before had she seen a snowstorm like this.

"Positive. Now suppose you run back upstairs and get dressed. Breakfast will be ready soon and I don't know about you, but I'm hungry."

"All right, but I don't like this much snow. It was never like this in the city."

It was mid morning before the wind died down and the snow ceased to fall. There was at least two feet of snow on the ground with drifts of three or four feet, but the barn and the bunkhouse were both still standing. Orlena, who had remained close to her brother, sister or Mrs. O'Connor all morning, slowly made her way from window to window staring out over the vast expanse of white. Everywhere, in all directions, as far as she could see, there was snow. It lay on the bare tree branches, covered the roofs of the barn and bunkhouse, gave the fence posts white dunce caps, created mountains where none existed before, filled in valleys and completely obliterated all signs of the road, while the stillness that reigned was intense, leaving any sound muted and muffled. She shuddered. "Mrs. O'Connor," she asked, wandering into the kitchen where that good woman was stirring a bubbling pot of stew. "When will this snow melt?"

Mrs. O'Connor looked up a moment and noticed the disturbed face before her. "Ah, that is not a question I can answer, Child. Suppose you just trot out and ask your brother or sister. Tis sure it is that you'll get an answer then."

Triple Creek Ranch

CHAPTER 11

VISIT TO THE BAR X

Slowly Orlena trudged from the kitchen. Her brother was the first one she saw, coming down the stairs and entering the dining room. He had on heavy clothing and whistled merrily. Silently she watched him pull on his warm coat after tying a scarf about his neck. As he picked up his hat, Orlena repeated her question.

Adjusting his hat and pulling on his thick gloves, Norman replied easily, "Well, this snow might melt most of the way, but I'm in doubts that we'll see much of the ground before spring."

Orlena couldn't help sighing. She had always hated winter; the snow was always getting dirty, and the streets were slushy, and it was so cold and there wasn't anything to do.

For a moment Norman looked at his sister. "What you need," he said suddenly, "is something to do. Run up to your room, put on the warmest things you have, then come down. Hurry now."

"Why?"

"Because I'm going to show you what real snow is like. Not that slushy, grey stuff you get in the city. This here is real snow. Run along now and get ready. I'll wait for you."

Seeing that Norman intended to wait, and wondering what it would be like, Orlena obeyed. She didn't know what she would put on until Jenelle appeared at the door of her room with an offer to help.

It was a slow and rather reluctant Orlena that followed her brother out into the world of white. Pausing near the door, Orlena watched Norman seize a shovel and begin digging a trench through the snow in the direction of the barn. After he had cleared a few feet, he turned and called, "Come on, Sis. You can't experience snow from the doorway." He grabbed a handful of snow, packed it lightly and threw it at her.

Orlena gave a little scream as the soft, cold ball hit her coat.

"Come along or I'll throw more," Norman threatened with a grin.

Not wanting to be the target of her brother's pitches, for she felt sure that he always hit what he was aiming for, Orlena stepped down off the porch and into the trench, slowly following the little path and watching Norman toss shovel after shovel full to the side.

A sudden shout from the bunk house alerted the two Mavriches that the men were emerging from their quarters. "We'll beat you to the barn," Alden shouted, waving his shovel.

"We'll accept that challenge," Norman called back. "Quick, Orlena, run back to the porch and grab another shovel."

"I already have them, Norman," a sweet voice called, and looking back, they saw Jenelle carrying two shovels.

"Don't over work, Jenelle," Norman cautioned. "But we're going to need your help if we hope to win. Here Orlena, go behind Jenelle. She can take the top layer off, you get the next and I'll clear the rest. Come on now. All in one smooth motion. That's right Jenelle. Now you're catching on, Sis. We'll have to work quickly because they outnumber us." Even as he talked, Norman was working.

Orlena, having never shoveled snow in her life or had much experience out in it, forgot in the excitement of the race, that "young ladies" wouldn't do such work.

What a race it was. Any time Jenelle or Orlena paused for breath, which was often, Norman would quickly take their place for a minute, making the snow fly with such an ease of motion and such speed that several more feet were quickly cleared.

There were some shouts back and forth between the men and Norman, and Mrs. O'Connor, hearing them, watched from the window for several minutes. At last, flinging a warm shawl about her shoulders she opened the door and called out, "Sure and tis a hot pie I'll be making for the winning team!"

The snow seemed to fly the faster with this promise and the men from the bunkhouse grew so eager that several men started their own paths while the rest all tried to work in the front, and instead of lengthening the path more quickly, they widened it.

"Done!" Norman's shout brought a cheer from Jenelle and Orlena and a collection of groans from the hired hands.

"That wasn't fair," Scott grumbled good-naturedly. "You had Mrs. Mavrich."

Jenelle's merry laugh rang out across the snowy ground. "And who did you have? Only every man in the bunkhouse." And the mistress of Triple Creek Ranch tossed a snowball in the direction of the men.

"But we were missing Hearter," St. John protested. "We can't work well without him, you know."

By this time Norman had cleared an area around the barn door and opened it. Delighted nickers and whinnies came from the dim interior where the horses were waiting. "Come on, men," Norman called. "There are chores to be done. I see you can't shovel snow without Hearter, but I know you can take care of the chores."

A general laugh sounded and most of the men forgot the path and plowed right through the snow to the barn.

Taking her young sister's hand, Jenelle pulled her away from the barn. "Come on," she said, "let's take a walk."

"Through this snow?" Orlena gasped.

"Of course. It isn't very deep and I've been longing to get out in it. Mrs. O'Connor wouldn't come with me. She said it was too much cold and wet for her old bones. Oh!" Jenelle, having pulled Orlena along past the corrals, paused to look about. "Isn't everything just lovely?"

There was no answer.

"Come on, let's go to the top of the hill," Jenelle urged, starting forward.

In silence they trudged up the hill until they came to the top where they stopped and gazed around.

"There's so much," Orlena gasped, panting from the climb. "I didn't think . . . there could be this . . . much snow. Norman said we wouldn't see . . . the ground until spring. He was only fooling, wasn't he?"

Jenelle, herself slightly out of breath, shook her head. "No, he's probably right. Once we get a snow like this, it isn't often we see the ground again until spring. Sometimes," she added as she caught sight of Orlena's face, "the wind will clear the snow off right down to the ground, but that's out on the range where there are no trees to block it.

"I don't think I'm going to like it," Orlena said slowly and shivered.

"Let's go back to the house," Jenelle said quietly. "A warm dinner will taste good after our fun."

Dinner was just ready when Norman came in from the barn. He was limping slightly and Jenelle looked concerned. "You aren't overdoing it, are you?" she asked softly.

"No. My leg just isn't quite used to things yet," Norman replied as he hung up his coat and pulled out Jenelle's chair. "I'll just use it a little more each day and it'll get back its strength."

After the meal had begun, Norman remarked, "Lloyd is back."

Jenelle looked up from her bowl of stew. "How are things in town?"

"About the same as out here. I'm glad I let him spend

the night at home. He split enough wood to last them for several weeks in case he should get stuck out here. He's also arranged for one or two of the men in town to keep an eye on things. It's one thing for Connie and Charity to manage when the weather is mild, but now that winter's set in—" Norman left his sentence unfinished and turned to his bowl.

For some minutes the only sounds in the room were the clatter of spoons against the bowls and the ticking of the clock. At last Jenelle asked, "Is anyone going to check the cattle soon?"

Norman nodded. "Yep. A few of the men will ride out and check near North Creek. Hardrich doesn't think we'll get more snow tomorrow, so we'll head out then and finish checking."

"Are all of you going?" Jenelle asked. She was always interested in the movements of the hands on Triple Creek.

Norman shook his head. "I'm thinking of leaving Hardrich and possibly St. John behind. There's no reason for Hardrich to ride out in this weather when there's no need."

The dishes had been washed and Jenelle and Mrs. O'Connor were setting the last of the kitchen to rights when Norman sauntered in and leaned against the counter, his thumbs tucked in his belt and one booted foot crossed over the other. "Mrs. O'Connor," he began as the ladies turned and looked at him. "Would it be imposing on you if I were to take my wife away for a few hours and leave you here with Orlena?"

Mrs. O'Connor gave a sniff. "Imposing, he's asking. And sure it's Margaret Patrick O'Connor who came to be housekeeper and tis not likely I'll be mindin' bein' left alone with Orlena entirely. Tis right the two of you should be goin' off together sure. Take no mind of us for we'll be gettin' along indeed and yer supper will be hot when ye return for it."

Norman couldn't hold back a smile at the lilt of Mrs. O'Connor's rich Irish tongue. "Thank you," was all he said, but much to that woman's surprise and delight, Norman then bent and placed a kiss on her cheek.

Turning to Jenelle, he said, "How soon can you be ready to go, Sweet?"

Jenelle laughed softly. "That depends on where we are going."

"For a sleigh ride and a little visiting." Norman's eyes had grown sober while he talked, though he still smiled.

"I'll be ready in five minutes."

And Norman departed to hitch up the sleigh.

It wasn't until they were skimming over the road, snugly settled under a heavy bearskin rug, that Jenelle asked, "Where are we going, Norman?"

"To the Bar X ranch."

"Oh."

Norman looked down. He couldn't see Jenelle's face for most of it was hidden behind her scarf. "Do you think I'm making a wrong decision?"

"No. But it may be difficult."

"Why do you think I brought you along?" Norman teased gently, and Jenelle blushed.

It wasn't an easy matter to bring up, Norman discovered, after they had arrived and had sat and visited for several minutes. At last Mr. Ledford said, "I don't reckon you folks came all the way out to the Bar X just to pass the time with chit-chat."

Drawing a deep breath, Norman replied, "No, we didn't, Ledford. There's another reason." He paused and glanced over at Jenelle who was seated beside Mrs. Ledford. He was thankful that Elvira and her brothers were not in the room.

"Well, what is it, Mavrich?" Ledford prodded.

"It involves some books which came from your home and into mine and which I burned."

Mr. Ledford stared at his visitor as though he had

suddenly ceased to speak English.

Norman began again. "It's like this. My sister borrowed some half dozen dime novels from your daughter a number of weeks ago without my knowledge. When they were discovered she refused to tell who owned them, having promised not to, and I, not wanting to keep such poison on the ranch even under lock and key, deposited them all in the fire. It was only two days ago that I discovered the true owner of the books. Evidently Elvira has tried to get my sister to pay her for the books since she can not return them."

For a moment Mr. Ledford didn't reply. At last he did. "I'm not sure where you got your ideas, Mavrich, but my daughter doesn't have any dime novels. She doesn't read such trash. Your sister was no doubt only trying to put the blame on some innocent girl from school. I thought you were smart enough not to fall for such nonsense." Mr. Ledford's voice was rough and held a sneer in it.

Keeping his voice calm and even, Norman replied, "Then I assume your daughter won't have any objection to not receiving any money for the books?"

Something in Normans' quiet, positive manner, cast a tiny bit of doubt in Mr. Ledford's mind. He turned to his wife. "Emmaline, have you ever noticed Elvira with any dime novels?"

"Well, I haven't exactly seen her with any, but—"

"But what, woman," Mr. Ledford barked. "You know something."

Mrs. Ledford replied softly. "I have noticed that her grades in school aren't what they used to be."

For a brief moment, Mr. Ledford frowned, then on hearing footsteps, he turned to the door and called, "Elbert!"

A young man stepped quickly into the room. "You called, Pa?"

"Yeah, go fetch yer sister."

Elbert nodded and disappeared.

Norman, not wanting to be a witness of such a scene as he could well imagine in a house like this said, "My reason for mentioning this at all, Ledford, was to make it clear that my sister was not to receive any more such reading material."

Mr. Ledford didn't reply for just then the door opened and Elvira entered followed by her brothers. "You called for me, Papa?" she asked sweetly, nodding politely to their guests.

"Yes, did you lend Orlena Mavrich dime novels?"

The question caught Elvira completely by surprise. She blinked a moment and her face flushed. "Papa!" she exclaimed. "Why would you ask such a question?"

"Do you own any dime novels?"

"Dime novels?" Elvira repeated. "What makes you ask that?"

Mr. Ledford looked at his daughter. "Mr. Mavrich here said you lent some to his sister and he burned them. That is where such rubbish belongs. Do you have any?"

Quickly Elvira shook her head. "No, why would I want them?"

Then Edgar Ledford spoke up. "She does so have some. Don't she, Elbert?"

Thus questioned, the eldest son slowly, reluctantly nodded his head.

"Where are they?" Mr. Ledford demanded.

"Under her mattress, last I saw," Edgar replied.

"Fetch 'em." Mr. Ledford turned then to his daughter. "And you dared to bring such rubbish into this house and then lie about it?" His voice rose until it was a shout. "Where did you get them? Tell me!" He grasped his daughter's shoulder.

T

CHAPTER 12

UNEXPECTED SMOKE

By then Elvira was crying and between her tears she managed to say, "Cousin Agatha brought them."

Edgar returned with half a dozen books which all looked very much the worse for wear. "Are these all you have?" Mr. Ledford demanded. "Answer me!"

"Y . . . yes."

With one quick movement the books were consigned to the mercy of the flames. "Now tell Mr. Mavrich that you are sorry for ever letting such trash pass the gates of Triple Creek! Tell him and then go to your room. I don't have time to think of a suitable punishment for you right now."

At her father's stern words and harsh tones, Elvira mumbled some low, indistinct words and then fled from the room.

During this scene Norman had with difficulty restrained himself from an outburst at the rancher's hard words and callused dealings with his daughter. Now he rose, saying rather stiffly, "We've taken too much of your time, we must be off. Jenelle."

Jenelle had also risen, and after she had let her husband help her on with her wraps, she turned to Mr. Ledford who was still standing by the fire with an expression of great annoyance and anger on his face, and said, her voice soft and low, "Mr. Ledford, I don't think your daughter is entirely to blame for the trouble. Had you paid as much attention to her as you do to your horses and cattle, you would have known that something was wrong. You may know cattle breeds and horse training, but you don't seem to know much about the hearts of girls. Right now your little girl is probably up in her room with a heart that is bruised and hurting and only you have the ability to help her if you will." She looked over at Mrs. Ledford who had remained seated on the sofa with a pale face. "Emmaline, thank you for the tea. Do come to Triple Creek sometime and visit."

As Mr. and Mrs. Mavrich stepped from the ranch house, Elbert, who had slipped away as soon as Norman had risen to depart, came up leading their horse. As he handed the reins to Norman, once the couple were settled in the sleigh, he said, "Mr. Mavrich, please don't think that my sister is . . ." he hesitated, then added, "She just doesn't know."

Norman nodded quietly. "Have you tried to help her? Have you been praying for her?"

The young man shook his head. "But I will. Good-night, Mr. Mavrich, Mrs. Mavrich." He touched his hat to Jenelle and stepped aside as Norman started the horse for home.

It was a silent drive as the dusk settled around them. The sighing of the runners, the steady, muted tramp of the horse's hooves in the snow and the jingle of sleigh bells were the only sounds in the still, winter evening. Several times Norman glanced down at his wife who sat close to him, her head on his shoulder, but he said nothing for several miles. At last he spoke. "What's wrong, Sweet?" he asked gently. "Are you wishing we hadn't gone?"

Jenelle made a slight motion with her head. "That poor girl. Norman, how could a father so neglect his only daughter?"

Norman sighed heavily. "I don't know. I don't know the Ledfords that well. They only moved out here four years ago and haven't been very social. But, Dearest, I have hope for them."

Quickly Jenelle raised her head to look at Norman's face. "You do? Why?"

"Because of Elbert's last words. He said he'd start praying for his sister. He has always struck me as a young man of his word who never says things he doesn't intend to do. And I imagine that he'll pray for more than his sister."

They would have been more encouraged had they seen Elbert Ledford on his knees that very night praying for his sister and his family and pleading for strength to walk as a Christian should. And Norman would have been humbled had he heard the young man thank God for such an example as Norman Mavrich.

T

The morning was brisk, cold and cloudy, causing each breath expelled from man and horse to become a steamy vapor which hung on the air a moment before disappearing. Stamping with impatience, the horses tossed their heads, the saddles creaked and the bridles jingled in the frosty air. Nickers and whinnies came from the half a dozen horses saddled and waiting to be off.

With a last kiss for Jenelle who stood on the porch watching, Norman swung up on Captain's broad back and called out, "Let's get moving!"

The eager hands needed no urging from their boss to set a brisk pace through the snow, for each of them was glad to be off. It was a much welcomed change from sitting around the bunkhouse polishing saddles and mending bridles. The snow wasn't too deep and the horses appeared to take as great a pleasure in this trip as did the riders themselves, for they pranced and snorted, tossing their heads with satisfied noises and acting much like two year old colts.

Once they had reached North Creek, Norman called a short rest and divided the men up. "Burns and Tracy, you two take the south side. Circle around to Penny Creek and head back by way of the valley. Scott and Alden, I want the two of you to head west. You should be able to make it to Crystal Creek since the snow isn't too deep. Make sure you check those sheltered sides of the hills. That's where most of the cattle were last winter. Hearter and I'll take the north boundary. We should all meet back at the barn before it gets dark. Keep an eye on the weather as you ride though. I don't think we'll get more snow, at least not much, but if the wind picks up we could get some blowing snow and the temperature might drop considerably. There's at least one shack along each of our routes. Take shelter if you need to. Be careful and let's move out."

"See you back at the barn!" Tracy and Burns called as they turned their mounts and set off in their assigned direction.

"Hearter, let's ride," Norman sang out and with a wave of his hand to Scott and Alden, he turned Captain towards the north.

For some time Hearter and Mr. Mavrich rode without seeing any sign of cattle. At last a few of the large herd were spotted near a small pond of ice. A few scrub trees grew along the banks of the pond and the cattle didn't appear to be suffering, so after noting the place, the riders moved on.

It was the same way with Burns and Tracy, a few head of cattle were sighted here and there, but no large groups and none were in places where they lacked food. The two cowhands made good time and before long had reached Penny Creek.

"I'd say there was more'n a penny's worth a water in that creek," Burns said, swinging off his mount to give him a little rest.

"Wonder why they came to call it Penny Creek?" Tracy asked, dismounting also and breaking the ice off the edge of the creek with his boot heel so the horses could drink.

Burns shook his head. "I don't know, but I reckon Mavrich or Hardrich might know. Don't know why we never thought ta ask before."

"Reckon we were always too busy checkin' fences or roundin' up cattle. But come on. Scott'll give us what for if these horses are left too long in this cold and get sick."

The cowhands, both seasoned riders, knew when the weather was too cold for horses to stand around for long without blankets and were always as careful of their mounts as Lloyd was of Spitfire. A good horse was worth a lot of money to a cowboy and no one would needlessly run the risk of ruining one.

For Scott and Alden, the job was longer and harder because most of the cattle, cut down in numbers for the winter though they were, had decided that they enjoyed the middle of the pasture lands, and the two men discovered small herds of them regularly and it was past mid day when they at last came in sight of Crystal Creek.

"Think we'll find as many head when we start back?" Scott asked, dismounting and walking his horse slowly. They would make a loop and check the farther side of the middle pasture on their way back to the barn.

Alden shook his head. "I don't know. That's one thing about this first ride. You never know where you'll find the most of them. We may find more or they could be over where either of the other groups are."

For several minutes the two men plodded on down the hill towards the creek in silence. Suddenly Alden stopped. "Do you smell smoke?" he asked.

Scott paused and sniffed the air. "I think so. Where's it comin' from?"

Alden shook his head. "I don't know. Who would be out in this weather on the Triple Creek?"

It was Scott's turn to shake his head. "If someone were out, a fire would feel mighty good right about now. But I don't figure Mavrich takin' a liking to strangers in the ranch pasture." The sun hadn't come out all morning and now and then a frigid gust of wind would sweep down off the distant mountains, swirling small whirlwinds of snow to fling in the riders' faces.

The two men, sniffing the air, slowly continued their way forward. It was certainly the smell of a fire, but where was it coming from? There was no sight of any smoke. "Scott, do you think it's coming from the cabin?" Alden's voice was low.

Scratching his face a moment, Scott peered in all directions, scanning the sky for any wisp of smoke but seeing none. "Could be. Should we check it out?"

Alden nodded and quickly mounted his horse. Pulling his rifle from its scabbard on his saddle, he said quietly, "I don't know who it is, but we may need these."

The cabin was on the other side of the creek, around a bend and hidden from sight by a low hill. Riding as quietly as they could, the men advanced. As soon as the cabin came into view, they halted. There was no light to be seen in any window, but the smell of smoke was stronger.

A sudden nicker came from Strawberry Girl, and from somewhere near the house came an answering one. There had to be someone in the house. No horse would just appear at an old abandoned house in winter.

"I reckon they know someone's about now," Scott whispered, also drawing his rifle out and unbuttoning his coat so his six-shooter was within reach. "But I still don't see any sign of life."

"Me either. Scott, sometime we're going to have to cross the creek to reach the cabin. There's some trees just across from here, what say we cross now? We'd at least have some protection in the trees."

Scott nodded as another whicker came from the ramshackle building. "That horse," he muttered with a frown. It sounded hungry to him. Then he turned to Alden. "I'll keep you covered as you cross."

"Right." Alden was soon across the creek.

Scott urged his horse down the bank and across the icy creek into the shelter of the woods. There had been no sound from the cabin, no light, no movement; in fact there had been no sign of life at all in the old house and had it not been for

the horse and the smell of smoke, the men would have believed it to be deserted.

"Well," Alden began after several minutes of watching the house. "I reckon we'll just have to go up and find out who's there and what they're doing."

Scott nodded.

Boldly, yet with caution, the two men rode up to the house. There was still no sound or movement. Scott slipped his rifle back in the scabbard and drew his six-shooter. It was easier for close up shooting if need be.

"Hello!" Alden called out as they pulled up before the door.

There was no answer. Was there even anyone there? Perhaps the person had gone off for the day. But why would he have left his horse?

Strawberry Girl stamped her foot in impatience. She was obviously wondering about the delay and would rather not stand around in the cold much longer.

"I agree with her," Scott remarked with a nod to Alden's horse. "Let's go in and see what's up, take a look at that horse and head back."

Alden nodded. Dismounting, the men quickly moved to the door and pushed it open, their guns held in readiness should there be a need for them.

The room was dim and dirty. A few glowing embers were the only thing left of a fire and there was no more wood nearby. The whole house creaked and rattled when a gust of wind swept down and shook it, and a cold draft crept through the room.

T

CHAPTER 13

A FAMILIAR STRANGER

A low moan from the corner of the room startled Scott and Alden who both turned quickly. They could faintly see the form of a man lying wrapped in a threadbare blanket on a bed of old straw. The man made a restless movement and moaned again.

Quickly Alden hurried over saying, "Strike a light, Scott."

Scott struck a match, but, on finding no lamp, had to content himself with adding it to the coals in the fireplace.

"This man's sick." Alden turned from the stranger, having felt his hot face and racing pulse. "We're going to have to do something or he's goin' to die."

"Let me take care of the horses first. Won't take long and I'll see if I can't find some wood for the fire." With that Scott was gone back out into the white, cold world. Catching the bridles of the horses, he led them around to the small shed attached to the house. There he discovered the horse they had heard.

"You poor thing," Scott said softly, as he caught sight of the thin animal. "I don't know how long you've been shut up in here, but you're in good hands now." As he talked, he had quickly unsaddled the two Triple Creek horses and, not finding any straw, grabbed a handful of leaves from a corner and quickly rubbed them down.

"I don't know what I can do for food for you, boy," he

said quietly, running his hands expertly over the pitiful horse, "but I can at least give you something to drink." Taking his canteen, he pulled off his hat and poured the water into it. Holding it before the horse he urged gently, "Come on, boy. Here you are. This ought to help for now. We'll see what we can do in a little while."

The horse had evidently been without much water for he drank thirstily until the hat was empty. Lifting his head, the half starved horse snorted his thanks.

Scott smiled. "You're welcome, fella. Now I'd best be gettin' back to the house."

When he again entered the old cabin, he discovered Alden working on a fire. He had broken the only chair in the room and was trying to coax the small flames into a brighter blaze.

"I brought the blankets and your water," Scott said. "I'm goin' to go look for some real wood."

Alden looked up. "All right. How about that horse?"

"He's half-starved and mighty thirsty. I gave him my water."

Alden nodded, and Scott, with a quick glance at the sick man in the corner, slipped back outside.

It was difficult to find firewood when the ground was covered with snow and Scott had no axe; however, he did manage to scrounge up some and brought it in where soon a larger blaze was warming the old house. Together the men carried the stranger over near the fire, wrapped him in blankets and were able to coax some water down him.

"We can't keep him here," Alden said in a low voice. "He needs a doctor."

"I know," Scott sighed, glancing about the worn building and feeling a cold draft. "But how can we move him? It'd be no use trying to get the sleigh out here with the snow so soft and no roads."

For several minutes the room was silent save for the crackling of the fire, the whistling of the wind through the cracks in the walls, and the restless stamp of a horse out in the shed. The man moaned and coughed. "Have ta keep goin'," he muttered.

Alden lifted the man's head and tried to give him a little more water. "We'll be goin' again in a little while," he soothed. "Just rest and get warm right now."

Opening his eyes, the stranger looked at the two cowhands beside him and mumbled, "Take me . . . learned lesson . . . he's a good . . . deserved it." Then his eyes closed and he sank back into a stupor.

Alden shook his head. "We've got to get him out of here and back to the ranch." He was looking at the fire as Scott placed the last few pieces he had found on the blaze and listened to them sizzle and snap. "Do you think the horses can make it if we take him along?"

"As long as we don't put anything on that other horse. We can take the shorter way back. Mr. Mavrich won't mind if the rest of the cattle have to wait until tomorrow. Not when a man's life is at stake."

They sat quietly a few more minutes watching the dancing flames. Then Scott rose. "I'll go saddle up the horses and bring them around."

Alden nodded.

As Scott saddled the horses, he talked softly to them. "We're going back to the barn, but we'll have to take it slow. Your new friend isn't strong enough to go as quickly as you and one of you will be carrying a sick man. I don't know how long it will take us to reach the barn, but we'll get there, Lord willing. Come on now. Yes, you too, poor fella. Wish I had a blanket to put over you but we've only got two and I think your master needs them both." Gently talking, he had fastened a makeshift halter out of his rope and then, taking the rope and the reins of the other horses, led them out into the snow.

After tying the rope to his saddle so the new horse wouldn't start off on his own, Scott hurried into the cabin. The fire was nearly out and Alden was ready to go. Carefully the man was carried outside and with difficulty, gotten into the saddle. With Scott holding onto the stranger, Alden was able to mount up behind him.

"Go ahead and start off," Scott told Alden. "I'm just going to put some snow on the fire so the wind doesn't blow a spark into the room and burn the place down."

Alden nodded and slowly set off. He knew if he followed Crystal Creek a little ways he'd reach a shallower place to cross.

Only a moment later, Scott was in his saddle and following Alden's tracks. The new horse went along passably, and Scott surmised he had been well trained.

The ride across the open range was difficult with the sick man and horse, for the clouds had grown heavier and the wind had picked up. A few lazy snowflakes fell and Scott looked often at the sky with an anxious face. Not only was he worried about the sick man, but also about the horse. Silently he prayed.

Noticing the snow clouds blowing in, Norman Mavrich said, "I think it'd be wise if we just headed back to the barn, Hearter. It looks like a snowstorm might decide to hit this afternoon after all. We can check on the rest of the cattle in a day or so."

"Yes, sir," Lloyd nodded, then pointed. "Perhaps if we ride up that ridge over there, we could see if there are any cattle anywhere in that valley."

Norman grinned. He knew his young hand wasn't eager to quit the unfinished job and that the prospect of more snow didn't worry him a bit. "All right, lead the way."

Lloyd set off and in a quarter of an hour they topped the high ridge. A lovely view of snow covered ground greeted them, but no cattle. "Who's that?" Lloyd asked, seeing the forms of some riders down in the valley.

"Why, that looks like Scott and Alden!" Norman exclaimed in surprise. "What are they doing so far north and where, what—" he left his sentence unfinished. "Come on, Lloyd, something's not right." Carefully he started Captain down the farther side of the hill with Lloyd following closely behind.

Reining up beside his men, Norman asked, "What's happened?" His quick glance took in the strange horse and the blanket wrapped figure Alden was holding before him.

"Thank God you're here, sir," Scott said. "We found this sick man and his horse in the shack on the other side of Crystal Creek. He needs a doctor and the horse needs a blanket and food."

Norman comprehended everything at once and quickly issued his orders. "Hearter, give Scott the blanket tied to your saddle then ride as quickly as you can to the ranch. Change horses and go for the doctor."

Scott had dismounted and taken the blanket from Lloyd almost before Mr. Mavrich had finished talking. With gentle hands and a quiet voice, he spread the blanket over the horse's back.

"Here, Scott, if the sick man doesn't need another one . . ." Norman looked at Alden as he untied the thongs which held his blanket to the saddle. Alden shook his head. "Then let the horse have it," he finished. "He looks like he could use it."

Scott nodded and added the second blanket. "You go on ahead," he said. "We'll catch up." Taking out his knife, he cut a few slits in the second blanket and, after ripping his handkerchief into strips, threaded the strips through the holes and tied the blanket together in front of the horse so it wouldn't fall off.

"Come on, boy," he urged softly, remounting his own horse and starting forward. "Come on. We've got food for you in the barn and a warm place to sleep.

Up ahead, Norman, riding beside Alden, was questioning him about how they had found the man. "And you didn't find out his name?"

Alden shook his head. "No, sir. He muttered a few words that didn't really make sense and that was about it. We got him to drink a little water and did our best to warm him up somewhat with the fire before we started back."

Norman nodded. "I wonder how long he was out in that old shack," he mused.

"Well, there wasn't any food that I could find and the shape that horse is in—well," Alden repeated, shaking his head. "It's hard to say."

When at last the ranch buildings could be seen, Norman urged his horse ahead to prepare things, and by the time Scott and Alden reined in, things were ready. Dr. French had arrived only moments before and at his direction, St. John lifted the light form from Alden's saddle and carried him directly upstairs to the guest room.

Taking the new horse straight to the barn, Scott spent over an hour settling the tired, half-starved animal; brushing his coat, feeding him, adding extra straw to his stall and then fastening a blanket about him. At last Scott moved out of the stall and shut the door. "There you are, Boy," he said quietly, "you're already lookin' better. There's plenty of horses to keep you company tonight and I'll be around to check on you later." With a final pat to the horse's neck, he quickly checked the rest of the horses and then left the barn.

The wind was still blowing and snow was falling, while the light that had given evidence that the sun was still somewhere behind the clouds, had faded. For a moment Scott paused, looking about. There were lights in the ranch house, bright lights downstairs which shone out over the snow like patches of gold, while upstairs only a dim light could be distinguished, for the guest room was on the other side of the house. Turning towards the bunkhouse, Scott smiled. The lights were lit there too, and he could see the forms of his fellow ranch hands as they moved about. He gave a sigh of contentment and trudged through the snow to the friendly lights of the bunkhouse where he knew St. John had kept his supper warm.

Up in the guest room, Dr. French straightened and

turned from the bed. "He's got pneumonia and he's weak from hunger, not to mention he's suffering from exhaustion and cold." He shook his head. "You say you don't know who he is?"

Norman shook his head and looked again at the white face of the stranger. "No, a few times I've thought he looked vaguely familiar, but I can't place where I might have seen him."

"Well," the doctor sighed, "Not much we can do about that now. I'll stay tonight, and we'll see how he is in the morning."

"I appreciate it, Doc."

"Humph," Dr. French snorted quietly, but his eyes were soft as he turned to look down at his patient once more.

That night as Mr. and Mrs. Mavrich were in their room, Norman, sinking down in a chair to pull off his boots, remarked, "Jenelle, I've hardly seen Orlena this evening. I never asked her how school was today."

Continuing to brush her long hair, Jenelle smiled. "You had a few other things on your mind, Dear. I asked her how it was and she said it was all right but didn't seem inclined to talk about it. But I do wish you had been here to help her with her arithmetic problems. I'm afraid I wasn't much help."

Placing his boots where they went, Norman crossed the room. "You helped her with her homework?" he asked.

"Someone had to, you know," Jenelle reminded him. "Mrs. O'Connor was busy with supper and I didn't think she ought to wait for you."

Norman put his arms about his wife and pulled her close. For a minute he didn't speak, but then he whispered tenderly, his head bent down over Jenelle's soft hair, "I haven't told you this evening, Sweetheart, but I love you now more than I did when I first saw you."

Jenelle looked up, love in her eyes, and their lips met.

Triple Creek Ranch

CHAPTER 14

THE FIGHT

Orlena put out her light and crawled into her bed. The house was quiet, yet she knew there were others awake. Mrs. O'Connor or the doctor would be in the sick room and her brother and Jenelle had only gone to their room moments before. For a long time she lay staring at the window, her thoughts in a turmoil. It had been another difficult day and she had been glad that Norman had been too distracted to pay much attention to her. She wasn't sure what the note said which Miss Hearter had told her to give to her brother, but it probably wouldn't make him happy. The note still remained in her coat pocket downstairs. What if it fell out and someone found it? How she wished she had been able to conveniently lose it in the snow on the way home! But Mr. Hardrich had not only taken her to school but had brought her back again in the sleigh, giving her no chance. Should she try to slip downstairs and retrieve it? What would she say if someone saw her? And what would she do with the note after she had it? This was the first time she had ever been sent home from school with a note and, though she had worn an aloof and superior expression when Miss Hearter had given it to her, inwardly she had shaken with dread, trying to imagine what her bother would do when he received it.

As she lay trying to decide if it were better to leave the note where it was until morning or risk getting caught with it now, her mind replayed the events leading up to the receiving of the dreaded paper.

Arriving at school in the sleigh, Orlena had quickly climbed down and made her way inside, for she had no desire to mingle in the snow with the other children.

"Good morning, Orlena," Miss Hearter greeted her pleasantly. "How are you enjoying the snow?"

Orlena shrugged. "I'd rather it were spring."

Instead of telling her she should be thankful for a warm house to live in, as Orlena expected she would, Miss Hearter smiled. "You know, I like spring the best too. I love the flowers and the green grass, the baby animals that are everywhere, everything."

Setting her books on her desk, Orlena sat down to wait for school to begin.

"Hmm," Miss Hearter shook her head as she moved some things on her desk. "I thought I had that book." Looking up she noticed Orlena. "I find I have forgotten a book we need for school today. I'm going to just slip over to the house and fetch it. I won't be gone long." As she talked she pulled her coat on and stepped outside.

Hardly had Miss Hearter left than Orlena heard the door open and someone else enter the schoolroom.

"I see you can't even keep your promise!" a voice hissed, and Orlena turned to see Elvira glaring at her.

"I didn't say anything except to ask for some money," Orlena declared, standing up to face her angry schoolmate. "If my brother jumped to conclusions, it wasn't my fault."

"That's a lie," snapped Elvira. "Your brother came and told my pa all about it. I'll never let you read another one of my books again as long as I live!"

Orlena tossed her head. "I don't care."

"Where's the money?"

"I don't have it."

Elvira stepped closer. "You'd better hand that money over now or I won't let you copy anymore."

Orlena shrugged. There were others who would let her copy still. "I don't care. I don't have the money and I wouldn't give it to you if I did."

Now Elvira was greatly upset and, raising her hand, she slapped Orlena across the face.

Orlena wasn't quite sure how things happened after that, but before she knew it, she and Elvira were fighting.

Hearing the commotion, one of the students had looked in the window and yelled, "Fight!" Instantly the entire group of students rushed inside to witness the scene, shouting encouragements to one or the other. Charity Hearter had tried to stop it, but her voice was drowned out by the cries of the other children.

Into the tumult came a sharp, commanding voice. "Children! Girls, stop that at once! Everyone get in your seats. Now. That's enough! Orlena, Elvira, stop this instant!" Miss Hearter grabbed an arm of each and pulled them apart.

Elvira whimpered, "She started it, Miss Hearter. She wanted to copy my homework and I wouldn't let her."

"That's not true!" Orlena burst out. "She slapped me first!"

"That's enough out of both of you," Miss Hearter ordered sternly. "Right now I don't care who started it, you are both to blame for fighting like wild beasts. Now go to your seats. No, Elvira, I won't hear another word out of you." Miss Hearter let the girls go and walked up to the front of the room where she turned and faced the silent room of students.

For a long minute she stood in silence and the tension in the classroom grew. At last she spoke in a low, stern voice. "I'm ashamed of you. Did anyone try to stop the fight or were you all encouraging it?"

She looked around the room. Heads had dropped and all was silence. A timid hand was raised. "Yes, Julia?"

"Miss Hearter, Charity tried to stop it, but no one listened to her."

The teacher's face relaxed slightly. "I'm thankful to know

that someone knew enough to try and stop such a scene."

Orlena moved restlessly in her bed as she remembered the long morning. Miss Hearter had said not another word about the fight until she dismissed the students for dinner. Then, keeping Elvira and Orlena in, Miss Hearter had questioned them about the fight.

Each girl had given her own view of the morning's fight though neither one mentioned the dime novels, the real cause of the trouble. Miss Hearter had told them that if it ever happened again, she would have no choice but to punish them both. "Is that clear?" she asked firmly.

They nodded.

"All right then. This time I'm going to send a note home with each of you, but should it happen again—"

"Oh, it won't, Miss Hearter," Elvira broke in sounding penitent.

Orlena had said nothing.

Now she had to decide what to do with the note. Just the thought of it being in the house made her shiver. There had to be a way to get rid of it! It was snowing, suppose she was to slip downstairs and—no, someone might hear her, for the stairs creaked. At last she gave up the idea of trying to dispose of the note before morning, turned over and tried to sleep.

When morning came and Orlena had to be awakened by Jenelle, she had difficulty in opening her eyes, for her sleep had not been sound; several times she had woken up in a panic that someone had discovered the note. Each time had made getting back to sleep more difficult. Now that it was time to get up, Orlena was faced with the problem of how to keep the note a secret until she could get rid of it. What if she put it in the fire? No, it might not burn all the way and someone would ask about it. Could she lose it in the snow? Norman said the snow didn't melt until spring and by then it would be completely ruined. Yes, she decided, that would be the best way. Then she hurried downstairs lest she be late for breakfast.

"Good morning, Orlena," Norman greeted his sister when she entered the room.

Orlena nodded and took her place at the table where to her surprise she discovered Dr. French sitting where Mrs. O'Connor usually sat.

"How is the man, Doctor?" Jenelle asked as breakfast began.

"Much the same," the doctor replied. "We'll see what today brings. Mrs. O'Connor is a fine nurse and I'm holding out hope for the stranger still."

Norman sighed as he set his coffee cup down. "I'd sure like to know who he is and how he came to be staying in that old shack." Then he turned to Orlena. "Sis, Mr. Carmond told Jenelle yesterday that he'd pick you up for school today as he had to go into town."

"No, I can walk."

Blinking in surprise, Norman looked at his sister closely. "Orlena?"

"I can walk to school myself," Orlena said in low tones, her eyes fixed on her plate. "I don't have to be taken like a child." If she rode with the Carmonds she would have no opportunity to get rid of the note.

"No one had any thought of your age, Orlena." Norman's voice was mild though still a little surprised. "But I think the snow is too deep for you to be able to walk all the way to town and back again. Remember, you aren't used to this weather."

"I don't care. I want to walk," she repeated stubbornly.

Before Norman could say anything, Jenelle suggested, "Perhaps if you are ready before the Carmonds arrive, you can walk down the lane and meet them at the road."

To Orlena, who hadn't really wanted to walk all the way to school in the snow, this idea sounded perfect. "I'll finish getting ready right now," she exclaimed starting up from the table.

"Hold on a minute," Norman said, catching his sister's

arm. "Finish your breakfast first. You still have plenty of time." He smiled. Would he ever understand his sister?

Watching Orlena quickly start down the lane, Norman shook his head, remarking to Jenelle, "I've never seen my sister so eager to start off for school. I wonder what has gotten in to her?"

"Perhaps she is just realizing the wonders of winter and wishes to enjoy the day," Jenelle offered.

Somehow Norman didn't think so, but he turned from the window without a word, his mind moving from Orlena's unusual behavior to the stranger upstairs. Who was the man anyway?

Orlena didn't have time to bury the note in the snow as she had planned, for Norman had been watching her from the window as she trudged down the lane, and when she reached the road, the Carmond sleigh was nearly to the lane. Sighing with frustration, she let Mr. Carmond help her up beside Flo and tuck the robe around her. Why couldn't she get rid of that note, she wondered? How she wished she could drop it over the side of the sleigh. Feeling in her pocket, she grasped the note, but paused. Someone might come along and see it. They would most likely pick it up and open it. Then it wouldn't take long before it reached her brother's hands.

"Mrs. Mavrich," Hardrich's voice in the doorway late that morning caused Jenelle to turn around. "Is Norman anywhere about?"

"He's upstairs," she replied. "Go on up and find him, Hardrich. He might be in the sick room with the doctor."

"Thank you," Hardrich nodded and, after carefully sweeping the snow off his boots and dropping his hat on the kitchen table as he passed, the foreman made his way up the stairs towards the room where the stranger was lying.

His light tap sounded on the open door, and Norman

114

looked up.

Quietly he moved out into the hall. "What's up, Hardrich?" he asked.

"I'm sending most of the men out to find and check on the rest of the cattle. St. John is going instead of Scott."

"He think the stranger's horse will pull through?" Norman hadn't seen the horse since yesterday for he hadn't even been out to the barn that morning.

Hardrich nodded. "Scott has a way with horses. He thinks a good rest and plenty of food and water will be all he requires. And you know he's usually right when it comes to horses."

Norman smiled. He knew all right. That's why he had made Scott Triple Creek's wrangler; he knew the horses would be kept in fine health.

"How's the stranger?"

Glancing back towards the sick room, Norman replied softly, "Doc said he's a little better. I just wish I knew who he is."

"There's no name on anything?"

Norman shook his head. "The part that really puzzles me, Hardrich, is that he looks familiar, as though I should know him, but I can't recall who or where I've seen him. Maybe you should come and take a look."

The foreman followed his boss into the sick room and looked down at the pale, bearded face on the pillow. "Why, that's Mack Davis!" he exclaimed in low tones.

"Mack Davis?" Norman echoed in surprise. "Are you sure?"

The man in the bed made a low moan and moved restlessly. Dr. French looked up at the two men standing by the foot of the bed and nodded firmly towards the door. It wasn't a suggestion; it was an order to leave.

Neither man spoke again until they had reached the dining room where they could talk without disturbing the sick man upstairs. Sinking down in a chair, Norman motioned his foreman to also have a seat. "You're sure that's Davis?" he asked in disbelief.

Hardrich nodded. "Yep. Even with that beard I recognize him. I think it also explains why you don't."

"I reckon you're right," Norman began slowly. "I never was around him much. Too busy with school and work and then heading off to college. He was gone before I got back. Uncle had written me about what happened. I wonder what he's doing back here again."

Shaking his head, Hardrich replied, "I don't know. Looking for work maybe."

"Then why didn't he just ride up and ask instead of holing up in that shack and nearly freezing to death?"

Hardrich couldn't help smiling a little. "You would have had the courage to do that after you'd been sent packing perhaps, but I doubt Davis ever had that kind of courage."

Mr. Mavrich sighed and began drumming his fingers on the table. It was rather strange to have the man his uncle had fired for getting drunk too many times and starting fights lying sick upstairs.

At last Hardrich spoke again. "What are you going to do?"

Norman looked up and his fingers paused. "Nothing right now. Once he's on the mend I guess I'll have a talk with him and decide then. At least I know who he is. I wonder if he's changed."

"He was good with horses and cattle when he wasn't drinking," Hardrich commented. "But he just couldn't give up the bottle. Used to ride into town in the middle of the night to get whiskey." The foreman shook his head. "Only took a drink or so before he was ready to fight at the drop of a hat."

CHAPTER 15

BURIED GUILT

"Hiram tried longer than most men would have to bring him around, but he just wouldn't give it up. Well," he stood up, "I'd best be getting back to the bunk house and rustle up some grub for Scott and myself."

"No," a soft voice protested and Jenelle stepped into the room from the kitchen. "Stay and eat dinner with us here. We have plenty and—" she looked at her husband.

Norman at once seconded the invitation and said, "I'll go find Scott and tell him."

"I think he's in the barn," Hardrich said, adding to Jenelle, "It'll be a pleasure to eat your cooking, Mrs. Mavrich."

"Girls, we'll just drive over to the Triple Creek first and let Orlena off before we head for home." Mr. Carmond picked up the reins and spoke to the horses.

"Oh no, please," Orlena protested, "just let me off at the road before your lane. I can walk the rest of the way home."

"It's not a bother . . ." Mr. Carmond began.

"But I would enjoy the walk home. It isn't too far. Please." All Orlena could think about was getting rid of that note before it was discovered.

Hesitating, Mr. Carmond said, "Are you sure? I did tell your sister I'd bring you back again after school."

"They won't mind," Orlena pleaded eagerly. "I will be home much sooner than when I walk."

At last he gave in, but Orlena didn't relax until she was trudging down the snowy road alone. When she was sure that no one could see her, she pulled the piece of paper which had given her so many troubled thoughts from her pocket. For a moment she looked at it and wondered what Miss Hearter had written. Then, as quickly as she could, she pushed the paper deep into a snow drift along the road and gently brushed snow on top. It was gone. She heaved a deep sigh and started quickly forward. Now Norman need never know about it.

As she reached the lane leading to Triple Creek Ranch, Orlena began to feel uneasy. What if Mr. Ledford mentioned the fight to Norman at church on Sunday and Norman spoke to Miss Hearter? Maybe the Ledfords wouldn't be at church. A snowstorm might come up and no one would be going to church. But what if Miss Hearter had expected a reply to the note? She hadn't asked for any today, but what if she did later? Perhaps she should go back and read the note.

Turning quickly, Orlena retraced her steps to the place where she had hidden the note. But where was it? After digging frantically with one hand for several minutes, she gave up. "It's no use," she whispered to herself. "I can't find it. Now what am I going to do?" She sank down into the snow beside the road and tried to think of how she would get out of this mess. It seemed that everything she did just made things worse!

Suddenly she realized that it was growing late and that she had better get home before Norman came looking for her. Rising quickly, she shivered and started back towards the ranch, her thoughts in a jumbled mess. She felt more nervous and tense now than she had felt when she first brought the note home. Oh, what was she going to do?

The smell of a delicious, hot supper filled the kitchen, the dining room, even pervading as far as the front room and drifting upstairs to tantalize the senses of all in the house, except the sick man who still lay unconscious upon his pillow.

"How is he, Doc?" Norman whispered.

Dr. French shrugged, his fingers on the man's pulse. "He's no worse. If he doesn't grow worse tonight, I think he'll pull through."

For a long minute Norman stood looking down into the pale, worn, exhausted face of Mack Davis. "I wonder what he's been through and why he came back," he murmured. Then he turned and quietly withdrew from the room, thoughtfully making his way down the stairs.

Jenelle met him in the dining room with a worried face.

"What's the matter, Sweet?" Norman asked, placing an arm about her. "Don't tell me supper has burned."

"No, supper is all right, but I thought Mr. Carmond was bringing Orlena home today."

Norman nodded. "I thought so too. Isn't she home yet?"

Jenelle shook her head. "And it's starting to grow dark. Norman, do you think she walked home?"

"I'm sure Alex Carmond wouldn't let her walk all the way home alone through the snow. Perhaps they stopped at the Running C first to let his girls off."

"It wouldn't take this long though," Jenelle pointed out with a worried look.

Norman gave no answer but walked into the front room and pulled back the curtains. A lone figure was seen trudging slowly up the lane. "There she is, Jenelle. She'll be here soon, though I'd like to know why she's walking." He added this last more to himself than to Jenelle.

It was five minutes later when Orlena at last stumbled into the warm kitchen. Jenelle hurried to her at once. "Orlena, your dress is soaked, and so are your shoes and stockings. Come, let's get your coat off and then I'll help you change into dry things before you catch your death of cold." As she talked, Jenelle had swiftly removed the girl's coat, hat and gloves. "Come along now, we'll soon have you warm and dry."

It wasn't until Orlena was settled in an armchair before a blazing fire in the front room, a cup of hot tea in her hands and warm, dry clothes on that Norman had a chance to speak with her.

"Orlena, why were you walking home?" he asked quietly.

"Because I wanted to."

"Surely you didn't walk all the way home from school!" Jenelle exclaimed.

Orlena shook her head. "Only from the Running C ranch."

Norman frowned. "Why from there? I thought Carmond said he'd bring you home."

"He would have," Orlena tried to explain, "but I wanted to walk the rest of the way."

"Why?"

It was Orlena's turn to frown. How was she to answer that question? "Just because," she replied at last.

That answer puzzled Norman for he didn't think his sister enjoyed the snow so much that she would want to walk home all the way from the Running C. It seemed as though there had to be another reason. But what was it? Norman hesitated to push Orlena right then since she had just gotten home and sounded tired. He decided to wait.

Supper was over and Orlena had, without a word, carried the dishes to the kitchen and helped wipe and put them away. Her face looked troubled and now and then a faint sniff reached Jenelle's quick ears.

"Orlena," Jenelle spoke softly, "is something wrong?"

Orlena shook her head. "I'm just tired."

"Do you have much homework?"

A shrug was the only reply.

Jenelle looked concerned. There had to be something wrong for Orlena to be so quiet. Gently taking the dish towel from her young sister, she said, "Go in and start your homework. I'll finish up in here. Go on," she urged when

Orlena hesitated. "Just tell Norman I told you to." And she smiled.

Slowly Orlena moved to the dining room and sat down before her stack of books. She didn't mind doing her homework tonight. It might help take her mind off of her problem, but she didn't want her brother to help. He might discover the cause of all her misery and then things would only be worse.

There was no sign of Norman, and Orlena began to hope that he would stay away until she was through, but her hopes were dashed a few minutes later when she heard his steps on the stairs. Bending over her spelling book, she pretended to be lost in study.

Norman stood watching his sister a few minutes and then quietly pulled out the chair beside her. Reaching over, he gently pulled the spelling book away, saying softly, "You're not going to learn any words if you only stare at them without really seeing them."

"I don't have many words tonight," she said quickly, picking up the next book on the stack. Her brother's kind manner only made the sting of her conscience worse. "He wouldn't be so kind if he knew what I'd done," she thought, copying down an arithmetic problem on her slate and trying to figure out what the answer might be.

"How was school today, Sis?" Norman asked, watching her stare at the problem on her slate.

"Fine."

"I never had a chance to ask you yesterday how school was."

"Fine."

Norman fell silent. Obviously he wasn't going to get much out of Orlena that way. "Orlena, you're supposed to be subtracting those numbers, not adding them."

Shoving her slate, book and pencil across the table, Orlena burst into tears. Burying her face in her arms, she sobbed out, "I don't care!"

With a face showing his surprise and concern at such an

unusual outburst, Norman attempted to console his sister and find out what was wrong. "Orlena," he said gently, stroking her hair, "it's not the end of the world that you started working your problem wrong. It can be fixed. Come on now, dry your tears and we'll work on it together."

The tears and sobs continued.

"Come on, Orlena," he coaxed and waited for a response. None came. "What is really bothering you?" Norman's voice was gentle.

"Nothing!" She wanted to say, "everything" but she didn't dare. If only he would go away.

Jenelle, hearing her sobs, hurried in from the kitchen. "What's wrong?"

Norman shook his head.

"Shh, Orlena," Jenelle soothed, sitting down on the other side of her and dropping a kiss on her bowed head. "Everything is going to be all right. There's no need to cry about it. Do you feel all right?" When no answer except more sobs came, Jenelle turned to Norman. "Perhaps we should have Dr. French look at her. She might have caught a chill walking home." Her voice was anxious.

Norman rose looking troubled. "I'll go get him."

"No! I'm not sick!" Orlena choked.

Pausing irresolute, Norman glanced from his sister's bowed head to his wife's face. At last he said, going back to the table, "Orlena, if you aren't sick, then stop crying and tell us what's wrong."

The sobs lessoned and at last only a few shuddering breaths shook the brown head still bowed on the table.

Norman and Jenelle waited in silence for Orlena to speak, but when no words appeared to be forthcoming, Norman questioned his sister about the reason for her tears. "Orlena, what is wrong? I know something's not right. Was there a problem in school?"

"I . . . I don't want to do homework tonight," she whimpered. "I just want to go to bed!"

"That's not everything," Norman pressed. "Come on,

Sis, it'll be easier to tell it all now than to wait."

Those words frightened Orlena. Did Norman already know what had happened in school? What if Lloyd had seen his sister in town yesterday when he went for the doctor. Suppose he had told Norman about the fight! Oh, why did all this have to happen to her? Life was never this hard in the city. When she felt her brother's firm hand on her shoulder and heard him saying her name, she burst into tears again and sobbed out, "I want to go back to the city! I want Grandmother!"

At the cry, Jenelle's tender heart went out to the unhappy child and she gathered her in her arms and soothed her.

Norman could only look on with a troubled face, for he was perplexed as well as concerned. This was a side of Orlena he had never witnessed before, and he wasn't sure what to make of it. He didn't say anything until Orlena had at last gone tearfully up to her room. Then with a long, deep sigh he wearily made his way into the front room and sank down in his favorite chair.

Coming in moments later, after seeing Orlena up to bed, Jenelle paused in the doorway and looked at her husband. He looked tired and grave. "What is it, Norman?" she asked, going quickly over to him.

"I'm not sure." He didn't look up as she perched on the arm of his chair and smoothed his hair. "There's something more that's bothering Orlena than missing Grandmother, but I don't know what. She hasn't been like herself all day." He rested his chin on his fist as he stared into the fire.

"Then you don't think she's just extra tired from walking?"

Norman shook his head. "No. But even the walking is out of character for her. No, Jenelle," he repeated, "something is bothering her. I just wish I knew what." There was a long silence, and Mr and Mrs. Mavrich sat and thought and wondered. "She didn't tell you anything else?" Norman looked up at Jenelle.

She shook her head.

The following morning Orlena came down to breakfast with slow steps and heavy eyes. She hadn't slept well for the second night in a row which left her tired, nervous and silent. She didn't reply to Norman or Jenelle's greeting but sat down without a word and spent more time toying with her food than eating.

Mrs. O'Connor, bustling about the dining room gathering the dirty dishes after the others had finished eating, paused beside her chair and exclaimed, "Tut tut, Child! A breakfast such as you have eaten this morning would scarce feed a hungry bird. You've hardly touched your food entirely! Is it yer own fault or that of the cook this mornin'?"

"I just wasn't hungry, Mrs. O'Connor," and Orlena shoved her nearly full plate of food away. "May I be excused?" She looked pleadingly at her brother who nodded.

By mid morning Norman was convinced that whatever Orlena's problem was, she didn't want him to know about it, for she avoided being in the same room with him if possible and scarcely spoke to him. At last he resolved to try once more to get to the root of the problem. Mounting the stairs slowly, his hands in his pockets and his head bent, Norman's footsteps were arrested by the sound of a strange voice. It sounded tired but distressed.

"Triple Creek Ranch! Doc, you got ta get me outa here 'fore the boss knows!" A cough covered up any reply that might have come and then the voice went on. "But I can't stay here. Weren't comin' here. Jest passin' through . . . Boss won't let me stay. Ain't right he should—" Another cough ended the sentence.

CHAPTER 16

AN AWAKENED CONSCIENCE

Quickly Norman made his way to the sick man's room and paused in the doorway watching.

Dr. French was trying to settle his patient, but the man was restless and kept pushing away the drink in the doctor's hand. Glancing up, Dr. French noticed Norman and motioned him in. "Here, Davis," he said to the patient, "you can just talk things over with Mavrich. But you need to drink this first. It'll help soothe that cough of yours."

The former cowhand turned a startled face to Norman, completely ignoring the cup in the doctor's hand. "Norman Mavrich?" he gasped. "But, where's the boss?"

"Uncle Hiram died several years back, Davis. I'm ranch boss now. And I'm giving you an order: drink what Doc has and then, if Doc says and you feel up to it, we can talk."

Obediently Mack Davis swallowed the medicine though he made a wry face.

"Is he up to talking, Doc?" Norman asked as Dr. French straightened up and set the cup on the table beside the bed.

"For a little while at least. I'll be back later, Mavrich. I need to get back to town and see some other folks. Don't let him out of that bed and see to it that he eats when Mrs. O'Connor brings some food up. Though," he added, "I reckon Mrs. O'Connor will take care of that."

Norman exchanged smiles with the doctor as he picked

up his bag. He knew from experience that Mrs. O'Connor was able to get her patients to follow the doctor's orders.

Once the doctor was gone, Norman drew up a chair beside the bed and asked quietly, "Well, what's your story, Davis? What were you doing in the old shack back beyond Crystal Creek?"

"I was jest passin' through, sir," Davis began. "I'm clean broke an' I . . . well, I didn't aim ta do no beggin'. I nearly asked fer work at the Silver Spur—"

Norman interrupted. "You were at the Silver Spur? When?"

"I can't rightly say. Beginin' a winter I reckon it were. Least ways not long 'fore the first snow fall. Spent the night in their barn, but jest couldn't get up the courage ta ask fer work seein' as how I couldn't get work there after I left here . . ." The man coughed a little and then went on. "I had some grub an' I remembered that old shack. I didn't think anyone'd find me way out there. I was aimin' ta move on, but . . ." here his voice trailed off and his eyes moved to the curtains on the window.

"What have you been doing since you left the Triple Creek?"

"Oh, I found work here an' and there. I gambled some an' landed in more jail cells than there are months in the year fer bein' drunk an' disturbin' the peace. I tried my hand at gold minin', but I never got much color an' I were always hankerin' fer the sight an' smell of a cattle ranch. Always meant to turn over a new leaf, but it jest never happened. Then I found myself in this part a the country, an' well—" He sighed and coughed. "I ain't askin' ta be takin' on again, sir, I—" Another cough cut off his words and Norman stood up.

"I think that's enough talking for now," he said quietly. "You're not going anywhere else for the time being, which means you're under my orders, so get some sleep."

"Wait," the sick man begged, "there's somethin' I jest have ta tell ya."

"Only if it's brief," Mr. Mavrich consented. "You need rest."

For several minutes Davis appeared unable to say anything for, though his cough was still, he couldn't seem to find the right words.

"Perhaps you should sleep now and tell me later," Norman suggested quietly.

At the suggestion the man struggled to sit up and exclaimed, "No!"

"All right," Norman soothed, easing him back onto the pillows, "relax, it can't be that bad."

Davis swallowed hard several times and at last said softly, "I . . . I stole some money from your uncle 'fore I left the ranch. I ain't never stole again, less ya call gamblin' stealing', an' I don't know, maybe it is. I always wanted ta pay it back, but money jest never can stay in my pockets." He heaved a deep sigh as though a load had been taken from his shoulders and looked up at Norman. "I know ya can't keep a thief 'round this ranch, but I promise I'll pay ya back jest soon's I find work. I—" His slight frame was shaken by a fit of coughing, and Norman lifted the sick man's head and gave him a drink.

"That is absolutely the last word I'm going to let you say until you've slept," Mr. Mavrich ordered firmly. "Now obey my orders and get some rest."

Wearily Davis nodded and his eyes closed.

After standing in silence for several minutes watching the man, and noticing the grey in his hair and beard and the lines of a hard life etched in his face, the master of Triple Creek reached down and gently drew the covers closer around the thin shoulders. He shook his head. "A life without the Lord is indeed a hard one."

Over lunch Norman told Davis's story to Jenelle, Orlena and Mrs. O'Connor, ending with, "He's been trying to live his life without the Lord all these years and look where he is."

"He's at a place where he can receive help if he'll take it,"

Jenelle said softly. "I have a feeling that the Lord has led him back to Triple Creek for a reason."

Norman nodded.

Mrs. O'Connor spoke up. "Then he'll be staying on?"

"At least until he's well enough to leave on his own. I'm not hiring again until spring, but if he wants to stay here and earn his board and keep until then, I'm willing to give him another trial."

Sitting in silence, Orlena had listened to the conversation going on around her. Just the thought of what Norman had said made her mind spin with questions. Why would her brother let a no-good thief who got drunk and gambled, stay on at the Triple Creek? Why would anyone let such a man stay around? What did Jenelle mean about there being a reason for Mack Davis coming back? She frowned down at her plate in bewilderment.

Noticing her frown, Norman set his glass of water beside his plate and asked, "Orlena, is something wrong?"

"Why are you letting that man stay here when you know he's a thief?"

"Well," Norman began thoughtfully, "there are a few reasons. One is that he confessed and wants to make things right. I think that such a person should be given a second chance and an opportunity to lead a different life. Second, he's growing older and hasn't a cent of money. A man can't live long in the middle of winter with only the clothes on his back. Third, by giving him a chance to remain here on Triple Creek amid the Christian influences of the men, I hope he'll let the Lord change his life. Does that explain things a little bit?"

Orlena shrugged and pushed her food around on her plate. Did Norman really think people deserved a second chance, another opportunity to do the right thing? Would he think the same of her if he found out about the note and the fight? Should she tell him? No, she couldn't. He didn't need to know. She wouldn't get into any more fights at school and Elvira wouldn't even speak to her any more. She should just forget it all. But a little voice whispered, "What if he should find out? What then?"

"He won't find out!" her mind shouted and she jabbed at a piece of meat on her plate with such force that the plate slid and her water glass tipped, sending a stream of water all across the table.

Ejaculations of surprise and dismay were heard and Orlena once again burst into tears.

Glancing up quickly from the napkin which she had hastily used to stop the rapid flow of water heading in her direction, Jenelle exclaimed, "It was an accident, Orlena, don't cry about it!"

For answer, Orlena shoved back her chair, rose and fled from the room unable to stop the rush of tears.

Instantly Jenelle's heart was full of sympathy and she half rose to follow her sister, but Norman laid a restraining hand on her arm. "Wait, Darling," he said quietly. "I think I should go. There's been something bothering her and perhaps she'll talk about it now."

Norman wondered, as he climbed the stairs, what had caused his young sister to be so—touchy. He could hear her sobbing as he approached her closed door. Gently knocking, he listened for a response. Hearing nothing, he softly opened the door and stepped in.

Orlena lay on her bed, her face hidden in her pillow.

"Orlena," Norman spoke quietly, "I think we need to talk."

"Go away!" was the passionate reply muffled somewhat by the pillow.

Sighing inwardly, Norman sat down on the edge of the bed and placed a hand on his sister's shoulder. "Come on, Orlena, I know *something* is bothering you. What is it?"

Keeping her face still buried in the pillow, Orlena moved away from her brother's hand as she cried, "Leave me alone. I don't want to talk. My head aches and I'm tired."

"You'll feel better if we talk this thing out, Sis."

"Go away, I don't feel like talking." The tears had

stopped, but her face remained hidden.

But Norman persisted. "I know you don't feel like talking, but I must know what's going on. What is wrong?"

"Nothing."

"Orlena, you know that's not true. Now what is it?"

The tears started again. "I wish I were at Grandmother's!"

Knowing that wasn't the real problem, but only an excuse, Norman kept questioning; for fifteen minutes he tried everything he knew about persuasion to get Orlena to tell him what was troubling her, but he only received silence. At last he stood up. "All right, we'll talk about this later."

Orlena neither answered nor moved. If only something would call him away for the remainder of the day, perhaps she could think of something to tell him.

"You could tell him the truth," Conscience whispered.

"But he'd be angry with me," Self protested.

"He's going to find out."

"No he won't! He can't!"

"He found out about the books and discovered who had lent them to you, didn't he?" persisted Conscience relentlessly.

Springing to her feet, Orlena paced her room restlessly while her awakening conscience tormented her, until at last she was so exhausted, that she flung herself down and slept.

She felt as though she had just closed her eyes when she was roused by someone gently shaking her shoulder. "Orlena, supper is nearly ready. You just have time to freshen up."

Drearily Orlena opened her eyes and saw in the dim light of the room, Norman standing beside her bed. "I'm not hungry."

"Then I'll ask Dr. French to step in and take a look at you," was the quiet reply.

"I'm not sick," Orlena protested though her head ached and throbbed.

"Then you can come down for supper. You have ten minutes."

T

CHAPTER 17

"NO MATTER WHAT"

It was a quiet supper that evening. Dr. French had declined to stay, saying that his wife hadn't seen much of him for several days and, since Davis was on the mend and should not require his services that night, he would depart. Orlena spoke not a word and even Norman was silent. Mrs. O'Connor and Jenelle endeavored to keep up a light talk, but after several attempts, gave it up.

After the supper dishes were washed and Orlena, whose head still ached painfully, was about to return to her room, Norman, stepping in from the front room, asked, "Orlena, is your homework finished?"

Homework! She had completely forgotten about it. So busy had she been worrying over something she couldn't control that all thoughts of unfinished homework had fled. She hesitated. What should she say? The very thought of homework increased the throbbing in her temples and she leaned against the door.

She didn't need to say anything, for her very actions spoke for themselves. "Well, I'll make an exception this time and let it go. If we have time and you're feeling better tomorrow, we might try to work on it in the evening. But I don't want it to become a habit, understand?" Norman paused for a moment, watching his sister and noting her quick nod. Was she ready to talk? He didn't think so, and he didn't want to push the issue any farther tonight. "Why don't you get up to bed now, Sis? Good-night."

Orlena mumbled a low good-night and stumbled up the stairs to her room where she quickly prepared for bed and crawled wearily under the covers. Instead of falling to sleep at once as she thought she would, she lay awake for a long time thinking. She had to admit that Norman had been kind and not stern at all when he asked her what was wrong. "But he won't be kind if he finds out," she thought. Her mind shifted to the sick man in the other room. It still puzzled her that Norman would allow such a man to remain on the ranch. "If I were Norman," she thought, "I'd send him packing."

"But surely you wouldn't send a sick man out into the winter without any shelter to go to?" her conscience argued.

"Well, at least he'd go as soon as he was well. Or I'd have the doctor take him away as soon as he could travel. That's what I would do."

"What if Norman had sent you away or wouldn't forgive you when he found out you had opened those gates?"

That was a question Orlena wasn't prepared to answer and she turned her thoughts to that evening. She had been relieved to hear her brother wasn't going to make her do her homework after supper. "I'm sure I would have gotten every problem wrong and then Norman would have gotten angry and—"

"Has Norman ever gotten angry when you didn't lose your temper first?" asked that small voice which had been bothering her all day.

"I don't care," Orlena muttered, turning over and pulling the blankets over her aching head. "I have to get some sleep. I hope it snows tonight, so no one can go to church tomorrow." She was still worried about that note, but at last, with her mind still moving from one troubling thought to another, she fell into a restless sleep.

When Orlena opened her eyes the following morning, bright light was filtering in through her curtains and she lay blinking a moment. What time was it? What day was it? Suddenly she sat up. It must be very late and it was Sunday morning! Was her brother upset with her because she didn't come down to breakfast? Why hadn't anyone woken her up? She could still feel a faint throbbing in her head, but most of the ache was gone. Dressing quickly, Orlena paused by the window to peer out. There had been no new snowfall during the night, and the light of the morning sun caused the snow to glimmer and gleam like thousands of diamonds. Everything was still; still and quiet. It was as though she, Orlena Mavrich, was the only living being on the ranch. "What if everyone went to church this morning and left me because I didn't get up in time?" A tiny stab of fear shot through her at the very thought of being alone in the vast fields of snow, and she shivered. Rapidly she finished getting dressed and slipped from her room.

The door to her brother's room was open and she could see that it was empty. Almost on tiptoe, Orlena moved down the hall. Mrs. O'Connor's room was also empty. Glancing into the half open door of the sick room, Orlena felt somewhat relieved to see the quiet form under the blankets and to hear a low snore.

Returning to the stairs, she moved slowly down them, wondering if perhaps there was a note on the table telling her to take care of the sick man until they returned from church. When she opened the door into the dining room, Orlena cast a quick glance about the room but saw no note. On tiptoe she crossed to the kitchen, where the smell of breakfast still lingered; she peered in. No one was to be seen.

"They did leave me," she whispered to herself, a feeling of panic beginning to creep up her back. "I haven't checked the front room yet," she reminded herself sharply. "Maybe Mrs. O'Connor is there and didn't hear me come down."

Orlena was almost afraid to look into the room lest it also be empty, but at last, holding her breath to keep from screaming, she stepped into the doorway. There was no Mrs. O'Connor sitting with her knitting or the mending basket, instead she saw Jenelle sitting in her rocker before the fire with a book open in her lap.

Jenelle felt rather than saw the silent figure in the doorway and looked up. "Good morning, Orlena," she greeted her sister softly with a smile. "Do you feel more rested? Is your head better? I suppose you are hungry."

Orlena nodded.

Closing the book gently, Jenelle placed it on a nearby table and Orlena noticed it was a Bible. "Come along and I'll fix you breakfast. Did you happen to notice if Mr. Davis was still sleeping?"

"Well, he was snoring," Orlena said.

Jenelle gave a little laugh. "In that case I think he's still sleeping. Perhaps he'll sleep a while longer if his cough doesn't bother him. He was awake several times in the night coughing, poor man."

Soon Orlena was seated at the table eating a hearty breakfast; her trouble and anxiety about her secret seeming to have fled with the bright morning sun.

"When I first woke up," Orlena told Jenelle, who had seated herself at the table to keep her sister company, "I thought I had been left on the ranch all alone, it was so quiet."

"We wouldn't do that," Jenelle assured her. "It was a lovely morning, but Norman and I thought you could use some more sleep since you didn't even stir when I went to wake you this morning."

Looking up in surprise from her glass of milk, Orlena asked, "You tried to wake me up this morning?"

Jenelle nodded. "I tried, but you can see how well I succeeded." She laughed brightly. "We decided then to let you sleep."

"I thought Mrs. O'Connor would be here."

"She needed to get out, and I was feeling a little tired, so I said I would stay home this morning. Norman and all the hands went into town to church and took Mrs. O'Connor with them. It really is a lovely day," and Jenelle turned to look out the window at the bright world behind the glass. "If I hadn't felt so tired, I would have enjoyed the drive to town.

The talk of going to town had reminded Orlena of the note she had not given her brother and she fell silent and finished eating.

When she was through, she carried her dishes into the kitchen.

"Orlena," Jenelle said softly, "go ahead and wash your dishes while I check on Mr. Davis." When Orlena nodded without a word of argument, Jenelle turned towards the stairs thinking of what a change had taken place in only a few months.

Mack Davis was awake when Jenelle stepped into the sick room moments later. He looked at her in bewilderment for he didn't remember seeing her before.

"I'm Jenelle Mavrich, Norman's wife," Jenelle said softly with a smile. "The others are gone to church this morning. How are you feeling? Did you sleep well once you stopped coughing?"

Davis nodded. "I'm all right, ma'am. I hope my cough didn't disturb ya too much." He looked troubled.

"No," Jenelle assured him quickly. "Are you hungry? If you are, I'll bring your breakfast right up."

"I ain't wantin' ta cause you no inconvenience ma'am," Davis began. "It weren't my intentions ta come here 'tall an'—"

With a gently firm voice Jenelle interrupted. "None of that kind of talk, Mr. Davis. It wasn't your intention to come here, but I think it was the Lord's. Now, do you feel up for some breakfast?"

The sick man sighed and nodded. "Yes, ma'am. I reckon that would be mighty good."

The morning passed slowly by. Orlena wandered about the lower rooms of the house, restless and nervous, wishing she had someone to confide in yet not ready to trust her secret to anyone. When the church goers arrived, Jenelle had lunch ready and everyone partook with hearty appetites. Mrs. O'Connor said she would take the sick man his lunch as Jenelle and Orlena cleaned up the kitchen, with Norman pitching in to assist. It wasn't until the kitchen was spotless that Norman, about to follow his wife into the front room, paused and turned to his sister.

"Orlena, come in here," he nodded in the direction of the front room. "I think it's time we had a talk." His voice was quiet, but Orlena shrank from his level gaze.

Without a word she followed him. She didn't want to but knew it was useless to try and argue her way out of it. The best she could hope for was that he would accept her excuse that the snow and cloudy weather had made her nervous. Surely he didn't know about the note. Orlena was sure he would have said something about it at the table if he had.

Placing a comfortable chair near his and Jenelle's chairs, Norman waited until his sister had seated herself before taking his own seat. For several minutes the room was quiet; only the soft snap of the flickering flames, the gentle hiss of a log and the steady ticking of the family clock created a pleasant sound, a delightful, family atmosphere. Then Norman spoke.

"Orlena, what happened to the note you were supposed to give to me a few days ago?" His voice was quiet.

Startled, Orlena felt her face flush and she stared at her lap. So he had found out after all! Who told him? All that didn't matter now, Norman was waiting for an answer. "I . . . I lost it." The answer was low.

"On purpose or accidentally?"

What made him ask that? How did he find out? If only she had read that letter first and written a reply. Surely Miss Hearter would have waited until Monday before talking to him.

"Orlena?"

Instead of answering the question, she blurted out, "How did you find out?"

Norman exchanged glances with his wife before replying,

"It wasn't difficult. I knew whatever was bothering you had to do with school, so I had a talk with Miss Hearter after church this morning. She asked if I had received the note she sent home with you. Now, why don't you tell us about it."

"There isn't much to tell," Orlena whispered. "You weren't home when I came home and then were too busy with that man, and I lost it the next day."

"I was at breakfast with you that morning, Sis. You could have given it to me then. And Jenelle was home. Why didn't you give it to her?"

There was no reply save a slight movement of the shoulders.

Norman leaned back in his chair and let out a deep breath. If only Orlena would tell him the truth and all that had happened without having to pry everything from her. With a quick, silent prayer for guidance, he returned to his task. "All right, Orlena, suppose you start by telling us what happened at school that caused Miss Hearter to send the note home with you."

Shifting restlessly in her chair, Orlena was silent. Didn't he already know? Why was he asking her? If he wanted her to tell so that he could get angry at her, well, he could just wait! Then the long, miserable nights and days that had just passed came back to her mind and that tiny, uncomfortable voice whispered, "He's more likely to get upset if you don't tell him. Just tell him everything and get it over with. You'll feel better."

Her brother's voice broke into her thoughts. "We're waiting, Orlena. We can wait all day if we have to, but we're not going to leave until we get this straightened out." Norman spoke quietly but with a firmness that was impossible to ignore.

Somewhat alarmed by the firm tones, Orlena suddenly resolved to make a clean breast of everything. "I . . . I," she hesitated for a moment and then the words rushed out all in one breath. "I got into a fight with Elvira at school because she told me I had told you whose books they were, but I didn't and she called me a liar and hit me and Miss Hearter sent notes home with us and you were busy and I was afraid you'd be angry with me but it wasn't my fault and I didn't want to give it to you so I pushed it into a snowdrift coming home from the Running C and then I couldn't find it and I didn't know what Miss Hearter had written and I was afraid you'd find out and I couldn't think about anything else and now you'll send me away!" She ended the torrent of words with a burst of tears.

Jenelle made a move as though to go to the crying girl, but Norman caught her eye and gave a slight shake of his head.

Waiting in silence until Orlena had stopped crying, he asked, "Did it make you happy to keep the note a secret?"

Hesitantly Orlena shook her head, twisting her damp handkerchief around her fingers.

"Did you feel better when you lost the note?"

Again there was a shake of her bowed head.

"Orlena, look at me." Norman's voice was gentle.

Slowly Orlena raised her eyes and reluctantly met the grey ones which looked so steadily into hers.

"No matter what you have done, I love you and I will not send you away. This whole thing would have been so much easier and would have saved you a lot of worry and stress if you had only told me right away. I know I have lost my temper with you before and I'm sorry. But please, Orlena, remember that I love you and always will love you no matter what you have done!"

No longer able to meet those steady eyes, Orlena's own had dropped and her chin began to quiver.

CHAPTER 18

RELIEF AND A HISTORY LESSON

After a moment Norman said in a different tone, "I'm not going to punish you for not giving me the note as you should have done; I think you have punished yourself enough for that. However, I am going to insist that you write a note to Miss Hearter apologizing for fighting at school. I also want you to apologize to Elvira."

"But she started it!" Orlena exclaimed.

"But you continued it, didn't you? Didn't you?" Norman repeated the question when Orlena didn't reply.

Very reluctantly she nodded her head.

"You can write a note or speak to her," he continued. "And I don't want to hear any more about you fighting in school! Is that understood?"

Orlena nodded her head once again. She didn't plan on doing any more fighting. It wasn't worth while.

"All right then, I'll say no more about it, but I want those apologies taken care of."

A feeling of relief swept over Orlena when everything was at last out in the open, and she gave a long sigh and relaxed. The fire seemed cheery, the sunshine outside seemed to be casting its glories about with an added joy, and even the ticking of the clock had a friendly sound.

Into the peaceful quietness came Jenelle's voice. "Norman, didn't you ever get into a fight at school?"

Orlena looked up quickly in time to see a grin creep across her brother's face and to catch a half embarrassed twinkle come into his eyes.

"Twice, only twice. After the first time I didn't think I'd ever dare to fight again." He glanced at the two expectant faces and then with a slight laugh he asked, "Are you waiting for me to tell you about it? Well, I suppose I might as well." Stretching out his legs and folding his arms, Norman stared at the opposite wall for a moment before he began. "I must have been around eleven when it happened. We still lived back east then and I was attending a fine school. I had always gotten along just fine with all the other students until one day a boy named Bruce Walker came to school. He and I didn't like each other from the moment we set eyes on each other. To this day I'm not sure why, but we couldn't get along. We were constantly competing for the top place in our classes and we'd rile each other every day. Then one day things came to a head. I'm not quite sure how it all began or who struck the first blow, but that didn't matter, for both of us had been taunting the other to fight. School was over, but only a few had left the school yard. That was the worst scrap I've ever gotten into." And Norman shook his head. "I couldn't say how long it lasted. It must have been several minutes at least. Of course the other boys were shouting and cheering us on.

"We both got in some good hits and were rolling on the ground each trying to pin the other, but we were pretty evenly matched and there's no telling who would have won in the end if Master Ditty, our schoolmaster, hadn't pulled us apart.

"He gave us both a licking for fighting and sent us home. I knew I'd have to tell about the fight for I had a black eye and my clothes were torn and dirty. It was a slow walk back to the house and I was hoping Father would be working late that day because Mother was more soft-hearted than Father. But it was not to be. Father and I reached the gate at the same time, only I had my head down and didn't notice him until he spoke.

"He tipped my face up, looked at me in silence and then

sent me into his office. I knew I was in trouble just by the look on his face, and I was right. It didn't take him long to find out that his son had gotten into a fight at school and been licked by the school master. Now Father had always told me that if I got a whipping in school, I'd get another one at home. And I did. After that I vowed I'd never get into a fight at school again."

"But you said you had two fights at school," Orlena reminded when Norman paused. "What happened in the other one?"

"Well, that one wasn't much . . . he began looking at Jenelle with a smile.

"Go on and tell her," Jenelle urged. "I think she might like to hear it."

When Orlena nodded quickly, Norman began his second story. "I was nearly sixteen then and living here with Uncle Hiram. I worked on the ranch but also went to school. Uncle believed I should have a good education, and our teacher was a well educated man who instilled more than the three R's into us. I was one of the oldest students in school at the time. Many of the boys my age had dropped out to work on the ranches, but a few remained. A new family moved in shortly after the term started and they were rich and, well, from the way they acted, you would think they owned the entire Rocky Mountain range and everything west of there. There were two boys in the family; one a few years younger than I was and the other a year or so older. They were both trouble makers and bullies. I suppose it must have been a week after they first arrived when, during recess, I heard them tormenting someone. Coming around the building I saw that their victims were Jenelle and two of her friends."

At that point in the story, Jenelle interrupted and turned to Orlena. "I have three older brothers, but they had all finished school, and I had no one to protect me from the school bullies."

Norman continued. "It sure made me upset to see the girls being picked on and I guess I just lost my head, for two against one odds aren't that great sometimes. But I wasn't thinking about the odds, I simply told the boys to leave the girls alone or I'd make them. Do you think that threat stopped them?"

Orlena shook her head, her eyes wide.

"You're right, it didn't. Anyway, to make a long story short, we mixed it up pretty good, the three of us, and I was sure thankful for all the training Jim Hardrich had given me in fighting and all the hard work I'd done on the ranch. It wasn't easy to knock them both out of the fight but . . ." He shrugged and rose to add another log to the fire, leaving Jenelle to finish the story.

"By the time the fight was over everyone had gathered about including the schoolteacher. He didn't try to stop the fight but waited until Norman had pretty well subdued both boys before he broke it up. He kept all three in after school, but your brother didn't look any worse when he came out. He even walked me home. You see I had waited around to thank him for defending me. I don't know what happened after that. Norman never told me."

"What did happen, Norman?" Orlena asked as her brother resumed his seat.

He shrugged. "Not much. The teacher gave us a short lecture about fighting and sent us home with notes. I took mine straight to Uncle, handed it to him and told him what had happened. I wasn't quite sure what to expect. He listened in silence, read the note, looked at me and then said, 'Get out to the bunk house and have Shoran fix you up. Then get to your homework; we've got work to do this evening.' He reached out and squeezed my arm. Nothing else was said about it. So, you see, Sis, there may be a time for fighting at school, though I probably should have just gotten the teacher, but your reason and my first reason weren't right."

The room was silent for several minutes until Norman rose, remarking that he was going to go up and see if Davis was awake. Shortly afterwards Jenelle also excused herself, saying that she was tired and was going to go lie down for a spell. This left Orlena the sole occupant of the room.

She remained silently in her chair for a little while thinking about what had just taken place. Things certainly hadn't happened like she had imagined; Norman hadn't been cross or angry with her, though she knew he must be very disappointed. "I was going to be good," she murmured to herself. "I really was. What went wrong? Why can't I be as kind and good as . . . well, as Charity Hearter? Everyone loves her, but they don't even like me. I have tried to be good," she repeated. "And I will be good. I'll just have to work harder," she decided, tucking her feet up and settling herself more comfortably in the chair.

It was pleasant before the fire and she gave a sigh of contentment. Now that everything was taken care of . . . except writing those apologies. She didn't mind writing one to Miss Hearter, for she almost liked her, but apologizing to Elvira! That was a ridiculous request. Surely Norman wouldn't really make her do that. She recalled the firmness of her brother's voice. "He will make me apologize," she realized with a frown. Scowling into the flames she tried out a few apologies. "I'm sorry our fight got interrupted by the teacher." No, that wouldn't work because she had been glad Miss Hearter had come in just then, for she had been getting the worst of it. She tried again. "I apologize for my unladylike behavior." That was better.

In a few minutes Orlena grew tired of composing apologies and glanced about for something to do. She didn't feel like leaving her cozy place, and when she spied Jenelle's Bible lying on the table within easy reach of her hand, she picked it up. She had her own Bible somewhere. Grandmother had said it belonged to her mother, but it was packed away in one of the trunks that had been sent out from the city, and she hadn't seen it since. "Norman might like it, since it was Mother's," she thought, idly turning the pages of the book.

It was obvious that it was a well loved and much used Bible, for it was worn, had many verses marked, and here and there a pressed flower was to be seen. Orlena never remembered reading much of the Bible before. It had always seemed like such a dull book and those she had known who read the Bible were old, sour people who thought it was wicked to laugh. But the sight of Jenelle's Bible with its worn pages, the memory of Jenelle's bright, cheery laugh and Norman's hearty one, caused a feeling of wonder and curiosity to creep over her. "What is in this book that makes people so different and like it so much?" she mused. Her eyes, wandering over the pages as she thought, caught a few interesting words and she began to read.

That night after supper, once the dishes had been washed and the sun had set, Norman turned to his sister and asked, "Are those apologies written yet?"

Orlena shook her head.

"You'd better get to writing them then because I want to read them before you go up to bed."

"What for?" Orlena demanded. "Don't you trust me?"

"Should I?" Norman looked searchingly into Orlena's face until she dropped her eyes and muttered, "I'll go write them."

When she had gone, Jenelle, slipping her hand through her husband's arm asked softly, "What about her homework? You know she wasn't well, and I feel somewhat responsible for not finding out what was wrong right away. Don't you think we should send a note telling Connie why the lessons aren't done?" She looked up pleadingly into Norman's face. "Please, Dear," she whispered.

Gazing down into the upturned face, Norman smiled. "All right," he agreed. "I'll write a note. I'm also going to drive Orlena in to school in the morning. Would you like to come along?"

"I'd love to. There are a few things I'd like to pick up at the store, with Christmas coming and all. I'll find Mrs. O'Connor and we'll make a list." She was about to depart, but Norman held her back. "What?" she asked, looking up.

For answer he bent and kissed her.

It was another bright, clear morning with just a hint of a glorious sunrise tinging the eastern sky; the air wasn't as cold as it had been, and Hardrich predicted a few more days of sunshine. "But I figure the temperature is going to drop and be downright cold before nightfall."

"But no snow?" Norman Mavrich asked his foreman.

Hardrich shook his head. "Not for a few days at least. But when it comes I imagine we'll not see the sun again for quite some time."

"How do you know that?" Lloyd demanded.

"Almanac."

"In that case," Norman said, "I think we ought to see about bringing the cattle in a bit closer while we can. It'll be a mighty tough job if we have to take hay all the way to the south border. I've got to go into town this morning, but Hardrich, here's what I'm thinking . . ." and Triple Creek's boss and foreman stood talking for several minutes.

At last Norman turned towards the barn door but paused, then retraced his steps and halted before one of the stall doors. A whinny sounded from within and a dark head peered over the half door. Norman gently rubbed the horse's face as he asked, "How's he doing, Scott?"

From the next stall, Scott, having finished brushing the horse, stepped out and moved beside his boss. "He's coming along just fine, I'd say, sir."

"He certainly looks better than he did before." And Norman eyed the new horse critically. "He seems well mannered—"

He stopped suddenly, for the horse, with a nicker, had lifted his hat from his head. A general laugh went around the barn.

Norman retrieved his hat with a grin and added, "I started to say he seemed to have manners, but now I'm not so sure." He wheeled quickly. "Hearter, did you teach him that?"

Lloyd laughed, "No sir. I haven't done a thing with that horse."

"Scott?" Norman growled with a grin.

Scott shook his head. "No sir. That's a new one for me. I've never seen him do it before." He patted the horse's neck and spoke softly to him. "What other tricks did your master teach you, Fella? By the way, Mr. Mavrich, has Davis told you what the horse's name is?"

"No, he hasn't, but if he's awake before I head into town, I'll let you know." Then with a nod to his men, Mr. Mavrich put his hat back on and left the barn.

T

CHAPTER 19

MACK DAVIS

When he entered the house moments later, Jenelle greeted him with a smile. "You're just in time for breakfast."

"I'll be right in as soon as I wash up," he assured her.

When Norman informed his sister that he and Jenelle would be driving her in to school, she wondered why, but Jenelle explained that she had shopping to do since Christmas was only a few weeks away and there was no telling if they'd be able to get into town much before then. Orlena accepted the reason without question for, even had she objected to riding into town with her brother and Jenelle, she knew it wouldn't do any good to say so.

Before they left, Norman remembered Scott's question and slipped up to Davis's room where he found the man lying awake.

"Good morning, Davis," Norman greeted him with a smile. "How are you feeling this morning?"

"Bout the same, sir," Davis replied. "It was kind a you to let me stay here, but I reckon I ought to see if'n the doc can't find me a place to stay, maybe in town though I ain't got a cent a money and—"

Norman interrupted him. "Now see here, Davis," he said firmly. "I don't want to hear any more such talk out of you. You are staying here until Doc says you can be moved and then you're going to the bunk house. No," Norman shook his head, "I'll take no arguments from you when I give an order. That understood?"

The sick man looked worried and reaching up, pushed his hair back from his forehead. "But I don't want to cause no trouble—" he began.

"The only trouble you're causing right now is trying to argue with me," Norman smiled. "I don't have time for that now, I have to get my sister to school on time, but Scott, our wrangler, wants to know what your horse's name is."

With a dazed expression, Davis repeated, "My horse? You have my horse? I thought sure he'd died out there. Poor fella, I couldn't take care a him an'—" he coughed. "How is he?" he raised his eyes to Norman's face. "Will he be all right?"

Placing a hand on the sick man's shoulder, Norman gave it a friendly squeeze and replied easily, "Sure he will, with Scott taking care of him, but doesn't he have a name?"

"It's Shad. I found him on the range shortly after I left here, an' well, I found his dam dead not far from him with no brand. Reckon it must've been some wolves or somethin', so I jest took the little fella an' cared fer him. Named him Shadow 'cause he were always followin' me 'round kind a like they say a dog does. Them sheriffs always took good care a him when I were, well, when I weren't able to an'—" Another spell of coughing stopped the flow of words.

"All right," Norman nodded. "I'll tell Scott his name. Now you get some more rest. That cough of yours doesn't sound very good."

Davis closed his eyes obediently but opened them again as soon as Norman had turned to leave. Watching the straight form of Mr. Mavrich, the easy strides he took from the room and remembering the quick smiles that had crossed his tanned face, he muttered, "He's a good man. A real good man."

Pulling the horses to a stop before the schoolhouse, Norman handed the reins to Jenelle, climbed down and then assisted his sister to alight. "I won't be long, Jenelle."

"Where are you going?" Orlena asked quickly, stopping to look at her brother.

"Just inside to see Miss Hearter for a moment," he replied quietly. "Come on, you can give her your apology now too."

Orlena wasn't sure she wanted her brother going into the schoolhouse with her, but there was nothing she could do.

When Norman returned to the sleigh a few minutes later, he found Jenelle was talking with Charity Hearter. He touched his hat to her with a smile. "Morning, Charity."

The girl looked up with a bright smile. "Good morning, Mr. Mavrich." Then she turned again to Jenelle. "I'd better be going in, Connie will be ringing the bell any minute. Thank you for taking the letter to Lloyd for us."

"You're quite welcome," returned Jenelle warmly. "I know he'll be glad to receive a letter from Katie." She waved as the horses, with a jingle of their sleigh bells, started forward, impatient to be off.

The Mavrichs' day in Rough Rock was pleasantly spent. Jenelle completed her shopping and spent several hours in the Hearter home visiting with Lloyd's mother while Norman took care of a few things and stopped by Dr. French's to see if he'd come by the ranch and look in on Mack Davis again since his cough was no better.

Just before school let out, Norman went to the livery where he had left the horses, and hitched up the sleigh.

"Well, Mavrich," the livery man asked, leaning against the side of the door, "is it true?"

Norman stopped buckling a strap to look up and asked, "Is what true, Randolph?"

"That Mack Davis is back and stayin' at Triple Creek?"

Returning to the buckle, Norman replied easily, "Yes, it's true. Word certainly travels fast around here."

"Well," Randolph shuffled his feet and hesitated.

"Well what?" Norman asked.

"Well, I just heard some of the older men talking in the

saloon last night, and, well," he paused again over his favorite word, "they said Davis had gotten kicked off the Triple Creek years back."

"That's true." Having conquered the stubborn buckle, Norman straightened and settled his hat more firmly.

"Well, you're not plannin' on keepin' him around, are you? Not after your uncle fired him? I mean," he added hastily as he saw Norman's jaw tighten, "I mean after he's well and all, and well, . . ." his voice died entirely.

Drawing a long breath, Norman let it out slowly before he replied quietly, "I don't see how it's anyone's business around here whether or not Mack Davis remains at the Triple Creek or not, do you?"

Randolph, feeling a little ashamed of his inquisitiveness, hastened to agree. "Well, no, Mavrich, I can't say that it's anyone's business what you do on your own ranch, it's just that, well, some of the men were talking about what to do with Davis if he were to, well, try to get work here in town."

"You can just tell those who ask that if anyone has questions about Mack Davis, he can come out to the ranch and talk with me." Norman's voice wasn't harsh, but it was quite firm.

"Yes, sir. I'll do that very thing, sir!"

Paying the livery fee, Norman soon had the sleigh before the schoolhouse. A moment later the children came pouring out the door eager to be away from their desks. Upon seeing Charity come down the steps behind Orlena, Norman offered her a ride home. "We have to stop by your house anyway to pick up Jenelle. You might as well enjoy a little ride."

Charity's beaming face was all the answer Norman needed, for he knew Charity didn't get many sleigh rides. After tucking the robe around the two girls, Norman climbed in, flicked the reins and away they went. He didn't drive directly to the Hearter home but chose instead to give the girls a short ride out of town down a snowy lane.

Neither girl spoke until the sleigh was skimming back over the frozen, snow covered road towards town. Then

Charity said, "Mr. Mavrich, Lloyd said you have a new horse on the ranch."

"We do at that. Though," he added, "he's not the ranch's horse. He belongs to a sick man."

Charity nodded. "Lloyd told us about some of the men finding him. Is the horse going to be all right?"

Chuckling at the remembrance of the morning's encounter with Shad, Norman assured, "He sure is. There wasn't much wrong with him that Scott couldn't cure with rest, food and water. And here we are, ladies," he added, pulling up before the grey house.

"Thank you so much for the ride, Mr. Mavrich. I did enjoy it!"

Norman nodded and, after helping her down from the sleigh, touched his hat to her. "It was a pleasure." Jenelle appeared at the door then with her arms laden with her day's purchases. These were quickly stowed in the sleigh, Jenelle was helped in and the Mavriches were soon on their way back to Triple Creek Ranch.

Ŧ

The days that followed were uneventful. The sun shone in a clear sky and, though the air was bitterly cold, no new snow fell for the rest of the week. Orlena had no further troubles at school and, with Norman helping her with her lessons, correcting and explaining often with stories, she began to discover that lessons could be interesting. Her arithmetic was still a source of many tears and short fits of temper, but Norman's patience was commendable and Orlena was beginning to get a grasp on the subject which had caused her so much trouble and cost her so much money.

It was the following Monday that the blizzard Hardrich had been expecting blew in. For two days the wind howled and roared about the ranch buildings, while snow piled high in drifts everywhere. Visibility at any distance was impossible and the men had to use a rope stretched from the barn to the bunkhouse in order to take care of the chores each day.

Orlena, never having experienced a snowstorm of such ferocity, shivered as the fierce gusts rattled the windows and whistled down the chimney. At night she burrowed beneath the blankets which were heaped on her bed, while during the day she was a constant shadow refusing to remain in a room alone. She didn't mind working on her lessons for that meant that her brother was in the same room, and his calm presence reassured her.

"Tis a winter storm indeed. I've never seen the likes of it entirely even in the old country." Mrs. O'Connor moved from the window and shook her head.

"It probably won't last long," Jenelle said. "This kind never do. But when it's over the men will be riding out to check on the cattle."

Mrs. O'Connor clicked her tongue in sympathy. "It'll be cold riding sure with all this snow."

T

The snow stopped falling at last, but the drifts were high and the wind kept blowing fitfully as though unwilling to admit its days of being king were over. Norman was growing restless. As he was preparing to go outside and check on things, Jenelle came down the stairs. "Norman." He turned at the sound of anxiety in her voice.

"Sweetheart, I'll be all right," he chided gently, thinking she was worried about him going out.

"I know you will, but I wish you'd go up and settle Mr. Davis."

"Davis? What's wrong?"

"He says he's getting up and going to start helping with the chores. I can't get him to stay in bed. You know Dr. French said he wasn't to get up yet. I'm afraid his cough will only get worse if he does get up now."

Norman frowned and muttered, "Obstinate fellow." Then aloud he added, "I'll go up and take care of things, Jenelle. Don't worry." Leaving her with a quick kiss, he flung his coat over the back of a chair and hurried up the stairs.

As Jenelle had said, Davis was out of bed struggling to pull his clothes on when Norman entered the room.

"Mack Davis, just what do you think you're doing?" Norman demanded sternly, pushing the door shut behind him with his foot, folding his arms and frowning.

Davis glanced up with a cough. "I jest can't lie there in bed an' let the rest a ya take care a them chores. It's 'bout time I earned my keep."

But Norman shook his head. "No, Davis, you aren't leaving this room. Now get back in bed. Doc's orders were that you stay in bed until he says you can get up."

Slowly Davis raised his head. "I can't earn my bread an' butter stayin' in bed. I knows ya gotta check on the cattle, an' I ain't so sick I can't take care a—" A fit of coughing overcame him, and he sank onto a chair to catch his breath. "It . . . it's jest the . . . the talkin'," he panted. "I . . . ain't . . . used ta . . . it."

With another shake of his head, Norman crossed the room and began pulling the man's boots off. "Come on, Davis," he said firmly, "the only place you're going is back to bed. And arguing won't do you a bit of good," he added when he saw Davis open his mouth as though to protest.

The older man coughed as Norman helped him undress and then held a glass of water for him. Swallowing the drink, Davis shook his head while Norman straightened the blankets of the bed. "I ain't gettin' back in bed," he protested. "I've got ta work an' pay back what I took an'—"

"Now see here, Davis," Norman admonished, "who is the boss of this ranch?"

"I reckon you are, sir."

"And who gives the orders around here?"

"You do."

"That's right. And I'm giving one right now. Get back in

that bed and stay there until Doc says you can get up."

Wearily, as though he had no more strength to protest, Davis rose and allowed Mr. Mavrich to help him back into his warm bed.

"Now," Norman said, after tucking the blankets around the sick man, "I'm going to go get some hot tea for you. Then, if you want to talk this thing out, we can."

Davis nodded. "I reckon I'll feel better if we do, sir."

When Norman returned a few minutes later with the cup of steaming tea, Davis's eyes were closed. Pausing in the doorway, Norman watched him, wondering if he had fallen asleep.

Just then the man's eyes opened and he said softly, "I ain't asleep, Mavrich."

Some ten minutes later, Orlena, who had regained some of her courage when the snow stopped falling and she could once more see out the windows which weren't blocked by drifts, mounted the stairs in search of something from her room. On reaching the top step, however, she heard words that made her pause and listen.

CHAPTER 20

CHRISTMAS EVE

"I tried ta do better, Mr. Mavrich, I tried hard. But it ain't never did no good. Least ways not fer long. I guess I jest can't be good."

Startled, Orlena remained where she was to hear her brother's reply.

"We can't be good in our own strength, Davis. Oh, it may work for a little while, but not for long, not forever, and even if we could make ourselves good now, what about the times before?"

"Before, sir?"

"Yes, can you make your goodness of today make up for the wrong things you did last year?"

Orlena didn't hear any reply, but slowly sank down on the top step, her face thoughtful. What her brother had said was plain enough. Even if she was good today, that didn't change the fact that she had been "just horrid" for years. "Then I might as well not even try," she thought, leaning her head against the spindles of the railing.

Her brother's quiet, steady voice caused her to listen again. "There is a way to make things right, Davis. Jesus Christ came and lived a perfect life and then died so that we might be forgiven. He paid in full the punishment for any sin each of us has ever done. All you have to do is accept it."

"How can I earn His forgiveness, Mavrich? I ain't got

any way ta pay fer it."

"Davis, if Hardrich came in now with a bag of money that would pay for what you stole from Uncle, and said, 'I want to give this to you as a gift,' what would you have to do to receive it?"

For a moment no answer came down the hall to the waiting girl who scarcely dared to breathe lest she miss it; then, with a cough, Davis replied, "If it were a gift, I reckon I'd jest have ta take it."

"That's it, Davis. That's all you'd have to do." Norman's voice was earnest as he went on. "And that's all you have to do with the gift Jesus Christ is offering you right now: a free and full pardon for everything you've ever done that wasn't right. All you have to do is accept it."

"Mavrich—" For some time only the sound of coughing was heard and a low murmur of Norman's voice. Then, just as Orlena had decided the conversation was over, the sick man's voice came again, sounding tired, "Could He take a drunkard like me an' keep him from the bottle? 'Cause I sure 'nough can't do it."

"Yes."

"Would He want to forgive . . . me?"

"He said 'whosoever' and if that doesn't mean anyone, I don't know what does. All He asks is that you confess that you have done wrong and want His pardon. He'll take care of the rest."

"Mavrich, I didn't use ta think there were anythin' in religion, least ways not till I first came here ta Triple Creek. But somehow yer uncle was differn't 'n most folks I knowed. I ain't never forgot him." He coughed. "An' now bein' here again an' seein' you an' the missus, well, I reckon I know what yer sayin' is true. I ain't worth anyone dyin' fer, but I'm sick a tryin' ta be good myself an' I—" here he was once again interrupted by his cough. "I . . . accept," he gasped out between coughs. "I . . . accept."

At the sound of a chair scraping the floor, Orlena rose hastily and walked quickly down the stairs, completely forgetting what she had gone up to get.

The rest of the day she walked around silently, and several times Norman discovered her standing with a far off look on her face which quickly disappeared if anyone spoke to her. Orlena had never really heard the truth of the saving grace of God shared so clearly, in such a way that she could not only understand it but found it hard to get away from. Even when she pushed it to the back of her mind and tried to forget it, it would pop up unexpectedly, seemingly without the slightest reason. There was a reason, however, even if Orlena didn't see it. The prayers which were offered up every day from nearly every member of the ranch for her were not in vain, and slowly but surely the Good Shepherd was drawing the lost, willful child to Himself, tenderly urging and leading each step she took.

The days passed by quickly; the snow, though it seemed to try, could not dampen the Christmas spirit which pervaded Triple Creek Ranch. Jenelle and Mrs. O'Connor were busy baking in the kitchen, causing the delightful and tantalizing smells of cookies, breads and other mouthwatering delicacies to pervade the house to the extent that the men from the bunkhouse found ample excuses to visit the ranch house several times during the day, in hopes of sampling a tasty morsel.

Not only was the house full of good smells but also of Christmas carols which could be heard any hour of the day. Never had Orlena witnessed such preparations for Christmas. Always before, when she had lived with Grandmother, the servants had done everything and all that was ever required of her was to attend the Christmas Eve service at church and again on Christmas morning, if the weather wasn't too cold and stormy, partake of the elaborate dinner on Christmas day and open her gifts. True, she had also done a little shopping to purchase gifts for Grandmother and a few of her most intimate friends, but never had she been pulled right into the midst of things as she was at the ranch. So contagious was the merry spirit at Triple Creek that Orlena made no objections to stirring batter, sweeping the floors, or even adding more wood to the cookstove.

Day followed day in a cheerful bustle of preparations. Mack Davis, being allowed by Dr. French to get out of bed at last, if he took things easy, delighted in sitting near the fireplace with some wood and his pocketknife, whittling away while he listened to the pleasant sounds and enjoyed the delightful smells.

When Christmas was only two days away, Norman set off with some of the men to check on the cattle and see if he couldn't find a Christmas tree. When the men retuned in the evening, they brought with them a good sized tree which brought exclamations of delight from Jenelle.

"Oh, it's such a lovely tree!" she exclaimed, clasping her hands. "Where did you find it? Do you think we could set it up tonight?"

"I think we'd better put it in the barn tonight, Jenelle," Norman smiled. "It's covered with snow. A night in the barn will give it a chance to melt so it doesn't leave pools of water on your floor. We'll bring it in first thing tomorrow morning," he promised before he helped Lloyd drag the tree to the barn.

True to his promise, as soon as breakfast was over, Norman and St. John brought the tree in and stood it up in the front room.

"Oh," Jenelle sighed, clasping her hands, "it's just perfect! Where ever did you find such a tree?"

Before Norman had a chance to answer, Lloyd's voice called from the dining room, "I'm ready to leave, Mr. Mavrich."

Quickly Norman and Jenelle, leaving Mrs. O'Connor, St. John and Orlena looking at the tree, hurried to the dining room.

"Oh, Lloyd, can you take a few things with you?" Jenelle asked.

"Yes, ma'am, I reckon I can. I'm traveling pretty light right now and Spitfire won't mind a little extra weight."

"Good. It will only take a minute to get them," and she slipped from the room.

Taking off his coat, Norman hung it up, remarking, "Don't worry about getting back here the day after Christmas, Hearter. Since we've got the cattle moved closer, we can handle the chores for a few days without you."

"Thank you, sir." Lloyd held his hat in his hands. "I know it means a lot to Ma when I can stay around a few days at Christmas time."

Just then Jenelle reappeared with a carefully wrapped parcel. "Give this to your mother and don't drop it in the snow," she instructed with a smile.

"Yes, ma'am. No, ma'am, I won't. I'll go put it right in my saddlebag."

"And Lloyd."

The young hand turned at the door, his hat already back on his head.

"Merry Christmas!"

"Merry Christmas to you too, Mrs. Mavrich." After shaking hands with Norman, Lloyd hurried out into the white world. Light snow was drifting down from the grey sky as he swung up on his impatient horse, after safely tucking Jenelle's package in the saddlebag, and with a final farewell rode off towards town.

"I hope the snow doesn't hold him up," Jenelle remarked, leaning against her husband as they stood together and watched the mounted figure through the falling flakes of snow. "You don't think there will be a storm soon, do you?"

Putting his arm about her, Norman replied easily, "No, but I thought it was a good idea to send him off this morning just in case.

"I'm glad you did. It would be such a disappointment for his mother and sisters if he couldn't make it for Christmas because a blizzard stopped him."

Norman agreed and then added, "Come on. It's too cold to be standing out here. Let's get back inside—"

"And decorate the tree," Jenelle finished.

$$T$$

A cheery hubbub of noise filled the ranch house the late afternoon before Christmas. In the kitchen, Mrs. O'Connor, Jenelle and St. John were all hard at work preparing the supper while the rest of the hands, along with Mack Davis and Norman, were gathered in the front room swapping stories, admiring the gaily decorated tree in the corner and enjoying the roaring fire in the fireplace. Carefully setting the china dishes on the table, Orlena paused to admire the delicate design on each dish. She had never seen them used before and relished the thought of eating off of real china again. At first she had glowered when Jenelle asked her to set the table, but when the dishes she was to use were brought forth, her disgusted mood vanished. Painstakingly she set the dishes around the large table. "Real linen napkins are to be used tonight, as well as solid silver utensils," she thought with great satisfaction. "This is how a Mavrich should eat."

When the table was finally set, Orlena stepped back and gazed with a critical eye. What was missing? Certainly the dishes of steaming food, but wasn't there something else? The candlesticks gleamed from the polishing they had received, each fork, spoon and knife were set in just the right place, even the carving knife set before Norman's chair flashed back a sparkle of light. Suddenly she knew. Quickly slipping from the room, she returned a moment later and with deft fingers arranged wreaths of pine branches to place around each candlestick, nestling a few gilded pinecones among the sweet-smelling boughs of green. With a smile, Orlena next scattered small sprigs of holly about the table, being careful to leave plenty of room for the dishes. This done she again stepped back and admired her work. It was pretty; the green and red of the holly and pine branches added a festive touch of color to the white cloth, gleaming dishes and sparkling candlesticks.

"Tis a pretty sight entirely."

Mrs. O'Connor's sudden words startled Orlena and she turned quickly, her cheeks flushing at the unexpected praise. "Do you really think so?" she asked.

"Indeed and I do," was the quick and hearty answer. "It's a table that would make yer grandmother proud to be sure."

Before either one had a chance to say more, Jenelle called, "Mrs. O'Connor, is the table set?"

"It is indeed and a prettier one I never saw."

At these words, Jenelle hurried to the doorway. On catching sight of the table, she gave a gasp and exclaimed, "Mrs. O'Connor!"

"Tis not me ye should be praisin', it's nothing I had to do with it entirely."

Jenelle turned bright, astonished eyes on her young sister. "Orlena? Why, Dear, it's the most beautiful Christmas Eve table I've ever seen. Thank you!" and wrapping her arms around the somewhat abashed Orlena, she pulled her close and kissed her.

Quickly the steaming dishes were set on and the men were called. Many were the exclamations of approval at the meal set before them and the look of the table. It was with hearty appetites that everyone dug in, and before long all that was left of the feast was a memory.

Leaning back in his chair, Norman listened to the talk around him for several minutes before interrupting it. "All right," he said glancing around the table.

Instant silence followed his quiet words and every eye turned to the head of the table, for when Mr. Mavrich spoke, every hand listened.

"We are all going to head into town for the Christmas Eve service in two hours, so everyone get ready."

"But the dishes, Norman," Jenelle protested softly. "They'll be much harder to wash if they are left."

"All right, pick a few helpers and I'll send the rest off."

Jenelle looked down at her fine china which had been her grandmother's and then glanced over at Mrs. O'Connor. "If you would lend a hand, Mrs. O'Connor, Orlena and I can get them done quickly," she replied.

Nodding, Norman issued orders. "You men see if you can get the chores taken care of by the time we finish with the dishes. Scott, Burns, see that the sleighs are ready and the horses hitched up in time."

"Mavrich," Hardrich asked before stepping outside after the men, "do you want anyone remaining here or are we all going?"

"We'll all go," Norman answered quietly. "Dr. French gave leave for Davis to attend provided he's kept warm."

Clouds raced across the dark sky, first hiding the bright, twinkling stars then letting them be seen again for a moment before another cloud, racing from the blowing wind, once more obscured them from sight. The sighing of the runners on the sleigh, the jingle of the harnesses and the merry ringing of the sleigh bells were the only sounds to be heard in the still, winter night, until they reached the outskirts of Rough Rock and the church bell began to peal out across the snowy streets, calling the townsfolk and ranchers to come celebrate the birth of Jesus Christ.

As Orlena followed her brother and sister into the church, she felt an awe begin to steal over her that she had never experienced before. It was the same old, wooden church with hard, rough seats and no stained glass windows, but in each window a garland of evergreen lay on the sill with a tall candle, its flame flickering in the winter drafts from the opening door, standing straight and tall in the center.

CHAPTER 21

THE BEST GIFT

The light in the room was dim, for no one had lit the gas lamps.

It was a service Orlena never forgot. For the first time she listened with great interest to the often told, yet still wonderful, story which never becomes old. For the first time she really listened to the carols being sung and felt again a love she couldn't quite understand.

In silence she rode home in the sleigh and quietly made her way up to her room. She hadn't noticed the falling flakes of snow, nor Norman's puzzled face when his good-night hadn't been returned. In truth, Orlena hadn't heard her brother bid her good-night; her thoughts were still in Bethlehem at the side of a manger where a new born baby lay sleeping; a baby who would grow up to die for Orlena Mavrich and pay for every wrong thing she had ever done. Was it any wonder that she gave no answer to her brother?

"Norman," Jenelle asked softly, standing near the window and staring out into the quietly falling snow, "do you think . . ."

Pausing with one boot half way off, Norman looked up quizzically. "Sometimes I think," he replied lightly. "Right now I'm thinking that we might have a regular blizzard by morning."

When no answer came, Norman's face grew sober, and setting his boots against the wall, he moved softly across the room. "What is it, Sweet? What's bothering you on Christmas Eve?" He put his hands gently on her shoulders and turned her around.

For a moment Jenelle couldn't seem to find the words she wanted for she hesitated, her brow furrowed and an almost troubled look on her face. At last, lifting her head, she asked, "Do you think something is bothering Orlena? She's been so quiet for several days and tonight she hardly said a word. Oh, Norman, I'm worried!" Her face dropped, and she drew a quivering breath.

Drawing his little wife close, Norman's arms tightened about her shoulders. "I don't know what's bothering my sister," he said softly, "and I agree that she hasn't been herself, but I don't think worrying is going to do any good. Instead, let's get down on our knees and pray for her. The Lord may be working. I've never seen her as attentive as she was tonight. Come on, Darling, let's take our sister to the Savior."

When Norman rose on Christmas morning, he found that he had been right; a blizzard had blown in during the early morning hours and there would be no going to town for a Christmas service. "I reckon we can just have one here as well as in town," he remarked softly to himself.

"What was that?" Jenelle yawned, turning over in bed and opening her eyes to find Norman dressed and by the window.

At the sound of her voice, he turned. "Merry Christmas, Darling," he greeted her, stepping to the bed where he bent and gave her a kiss. "Oh, I was just remarking to myself that we can have our Christmas service right here."

Pushing herself up, Jenelle asked, "Why?"

"Blizzard," and Norman held open the curtain. "If you'd like, you can go back to sleep, since we can't go anywhere."

For a moment Jenelle sat and blinked then suddenly she

sprang up, "Why it's Christmas! Norman Mavrich, I'm not going to spend Christmas morning in bed!"

Chuckling, Norman hurried from the room to light the fires downstairs.

The morning passed by pleasantly in spite of the snowstorm outside. Norman held a small Christmas service for those in the ranch house and then the ladies began preparations for the large dinner of turkey, stuffing, gravy, potatoes, rolls and several other things, not to mention the pies and cookies for dessert.

"We'll never be able to eat all this," Orlena remarked, looking about the crowded kitchen. "Not without all the hands. Are you sure they'll come?"

Norman laughed. "I'm more than sure. They may be half frozen when they arrive, but they'll be here."

He was right and an hour before the meal was to be ready, a great stomping and stamping on the porch was heard and in a few minutes the men entered the warm kitchen.

After dinner was eaten and cleared away, everyone retired to the front room to exchange gifts. None were costly or elaborate, but instead were useful items or occasionally something which produced a laugh. There was a great deal of talk and laughter; only Orlena seemed sober as she watched the merry making from a secluded corner. Had she been sitting near the doorway, no doubt she would have slipped away to her room. As it was, however, she remained where she was and watched. The gifts she received from her brother, Jenelle, Mrs. O'Connor and Hardrich were received with smiles and polite thanks, but though her mouth smiled, Jenelle noticed that her eyes remained pensive.

After the gifts there was much singing and many stories until at last, with great apparent reluctance, the men rose to depart. The snow had stopped altogether, the sky was a brilliant spectacle of gleaming, twinkling stars and, though the snow was deep and the paths cleared only the day before, the moon shone with such brilliance that there was no need for a lantern and the men plunged into the white drifts with laughter and calls of "Merry Christmas!"

As the shouts of the men died away, the ranch house became quiet. Davis retired to his room feeling more tired than he would admit and Mrs. O'Connor, worn out by the bustle and busyness of the last several weeks, bade good-night to Norman and Jenelle and disappeared upstairs.

Leaning wearily against her husband, Jenelle closed her eyes with a tired sigh.

"Tired?"

She nodded then added, "But it was worth it."

With his arm about Jenelle, Norman slowly crossed the kitchen and entered the dining room. "Let's put out the candles on the tree and bank the fire. Then we can retire."

"Where's Orlena?"

Pausing to push a chair under the table so Jenelle wouldn't trip on it, Norman shook his head. "I don't know. I expect she's gone up to her room, though she didn't say good-night."

Silently, with only the sound of the steadily ticking clock to be heard besides their own soft footsteps, Mr. and Mrs. Mavrich entered the front room where to their astonishment they discovered Orlena still curled up in her chair, almost hidden by the tree.

"Why Orlena," Norman exclaimed, "I thought you had gone up to your room. Aren't you tired?"

A faint shake of the bowed brown head was the only answer.

"Are you feeling all right, Dear?" Jenelle, slipping from her husband's arm, crossed to the girl's side and gently caressed the locks which helped hide the face.

A sudden burst of tears was the unexpected answer.

"What on earth—" Norman began in astonishment, staring at his sister with concern. "What is the matter, Sis?"

At the sound of his worried tones, Orlena sprang from her chair to throw herself into his arms while she sobbed out, "I can't do it either! I can't! I tried!"

Holding her close, Norman looked over Orlena's head at Jenelle whose face mirrored his own in bewilderment and pity. For a few minutes all he could do was attempt to soothe and calm the crying girl in his arms. When at last Orlena's tears lessened, Norman, gently pulling her to the sofa, drew her down beside him and asked softly, "What is it that you can't do?"

"I . . . I can't be good! Mr. Davis said he couldn't be good either. But I want to be!"

Sitting down on the other side of the troubled child, Jenelle silently prayed that tonight would be the night Orlena would fully yield herself to the Lord.

Norman was also praying, praying for wisdom in talking with his sister. "You can't be good in your own strength, Sis. No one can."

"I . . . I know," she sniffed, wiping her eyes with the handkerchief Norman handed her. "I heard you tell Mr. Davis that. H . . . he got help and . . . I want it too, but I don't know how!"

In quiet tones, Norman told the rest of the Christmas story, of how Jesus lived a perfect life and then died to save us from our sins if we would only ask Him to. "All you have to do, Sis," he said softly, "is confess to Him that you have done wrong and ask Him to forgive you. He will; all you have to do is accept Him."

There was a long pause. The fire had died down and even with the flickering flames of the tree's candles, the room was dim. At last Orlena whispered, "I want to."

"Would you like to kneel down with us here and do it now?"

She nodded and the three on the sofa slipped to their knees.

When they arose a few minutes later, Orlena drew a long quivering sigh and looked up. There was a smile on her face, a smile of peace and rest that Norman had never seen there before. Instinctively he put his arms about her and Jenelle as he said fervently, "Thank you Lord!" Then to Orlena he added, "This is the best Christmas gift you could ever give us, Sis!"

Jenelle was beyond words. She could only hug her sister while happy tears trickled down her cheeks.

The following day was bright and clear. The sun rose in splendor and caused the snow to sparkle and flash with amazing brilliance. Never had life looked so different and wonderful to Orlena Mavrich than it did that morning after Christmas. When she came down to breakfast, her smile was bright, and she felt so free that she skipped into the kitchen to greet Mrs. O'Connor and Jenelle before starting to set the table.

Mrs. O'Connor stared after her in astonishment for a moment before turning to Mrs. Mavrich. "What has gotten into the child?" she asked.

With a smile as bright as Orlena's own, Jenelle told of the night's joyous event.

"Ah, tis a right gladsome thing entirely and an answer to many years of prayers!" And the older woman dropped the spoon she had been using to stir the oatmeal and clasped her hands murmuring a low prayer of thanksgiving.

For several days afterwards life seemed all rose colored to Orlena, and even her daily time of study with her brother or Jenelle wasn't as difficult as it had been before, for she now tried to enjoy it. When she had asked Norman to help her find their mother's Bible, he agreed at once and together they climbed into the attic. There they remained and when Jenelle climbed up to find them for supper, she discovered them looking through an old trunk by lamp light.

"Are you two coming down for supper?" Jenelle asked.

Two pairs of startled eyes turned to look at her with such an identical blank expression on their faces that Jenelle burst into a merry laugh. "Why don't you bring that trunk downstairs, Norman, where you can look at its contents with more comfort."

"Oh, yes, please do bring it down, Norman," Orlena begged.

With a smile, Norman agreed. He hadn't looked through the old trunk he had brought to the ranch with him after his parent's death for many years, and seeing his mother and father's things brought back so many memories that, had Jenelle not called them, he at least would have remained there until the oil in the lamp was spent.

T

On the first day back at school after the new year, Orlena was rather apprehensive. She knew she would have to give up cheating and do her own work, but she wasn't at all sure she could. And what would her few friends say if she acted differently?

To her delight, Orlena quickly discovered that all the studying which she had done each day at the ranch had made it possible for her to keep up with her classmates without the need to cheat. At least she could keep up in every subject but arithmetic. She would have to work harder on that before she could even hope to attain the level of knowledge Charity Hearter and others her age had.

T

Days passed which turned into weeks and still winter kept its blanket of snow on the ground. Some weeks the sun tried its best to melt the mounds of white but, before it could succeed, another snowstorm would blow down from the rockies and often for days the ranchers would be confined to their own ranches. During that time life at Triple Creek passed by with more pleasantness and harmony than in the early part of winter, for Orlena was changing. True, there were still days when her selfish nature got the better of her or her temper mastered any calming thoughts or pricks of conscience, when days of gloomy weather with no sign of the sun brought on a moodiness which was hard to break, but she was learning. Reading her mother's Bible, Orlena often found marked or underlined verses; these she would read over and over wondering why they had been marked or discovering for herself a precious gem to help.

T

January disappeared into February, and March was rapidly approaching, when Lloyd rode up to the ranch one cloudy afternoon. He had been to town for a few supplies. On hearing Mr. Mavrich's voice through the open barn door, he dismounted and, leading his horse, stepped into the warmth of the barn. "I picked up the mail, Mr. Mavrich, while I was in town."

Turning from Alden and Tracy, Norman glanced towards the open door. "I wasn't expecting anything in the mail." Setting down the saddle soap and rag which he had been using, he brushed his hands on his pant legs before accepting the solitary envelope Lloyd had pulled from the inside pocket of his coat.

"I wasn't goin' to stop, but Mrs. Cannon mentioned there was something for Triple Creek when I was in the store."

"Thanks, Hearter," Norman said, turning the envelope over in his hands and trying to read the postmark, as there was no return address. At last he gave up and, pulling out his penknife, carefully slit the envelope and pulled out a single sheet of paper. A quick glance at the signature and Norman looked up with a grin. "It's from Greg."

"Greg?" Alden exclaimed incredulously, "I thought sure he'd gone an' forgotten all about us."

"Why, we haven't heard from him since he arrived back east an' then it was jest a line," Tracy added. "What's he say, Boss?"

"Yeah, when's he comin' back?"

"Maybe he's got to liking it back east, Hearter," Alden suggested, "and isn't comin' back."

Having rapidly scanned the short letter while the men talked, Norman looked up. "Oh, he's comin' back all right. Just as soon as spring is here, he's coming on the first train with his wife."

"His wife?"

"You mean ta say he's gone and got married already?"

"Thought he was waitin' till spring!"

Before Norman could reply, Hardrich, St. John, Burns and Scott came in. "What's all the commotion?" Hardrich demanded.

Everyone talked at once and at last Mr. Mavrich held up his hand for quiet. "If you all want to hear what else Greg has to say, suppose you keep quiet a few minutes." The men fell silent at once and Norman consulted the letter again. "As I was saying, he and his wife are coming back as soon as spring is here and he was hoping someone from the ranch," here he read from the letter, "could look us up a nice, small place in town. It don't have to be big but it must have a place to plant flowers as Mary is used to them." Pausing for a brief moment while he scanned the rest of the letter he added, "He said he'd wire us what train they were coming on."

"That's it?" Scott questioned, and when Norman nodded, exclaimed, "I don't know what that girl could have seen in him if his letters to her were as interesting and full of news."

The men laughed. "But you must admit, Scott," St. John put in, "Greg can talk a heap better than that letter."

Coming out of Spitfire's stall where he had been unsaddling and rubbing him down since the other men had come in, Lloyd remarked, "You know what I think. I think Greg probably reasoned that we wouldn't be interested in city life and didn't want to waste good paper and time writing when he'll be seeing us come spring."

"You may have something there, Hearter," Norman said, clasping him on the shoulder. "But I reckon we ought to be getting those horses in now. I don't like the look of the clouds in the northwest."

T

CHAPTER 22

RINGLEADER

Norman's worries were confirmed only a few hours later when a sudden, fierce gust of wind shook the ranch house, startling everyone and causing Norman to sit up in bed.

"Norman, where are you going?" Jenelle whispered as her husband began pulling on his clothes.

"Just to check on things."

Quickly she caught his arm. "You're not going outside!"

"No," he reassured. "I'm just going to check the house and look in on Davis. His cough seemed a little worse tonight and with this wind we won't be able to hear a thing."

Settling back on her pillow and pulling the covers close about her chin, Jenelle watched Norman slip from the room with the small, lit lamp and listened to the roaring of the wind and wondered how long this storm would last.

Pausing only a moment in the hallway, Norman moved first across the hall to his sister's room. There, after softly opening the door and carefully shading the lamp, he looked in. Orlena's head turned toward the faint ray of light and she whispered, "I'm awake."

Quietly Norman went in. "Did the wind wake you?" he asked.

Orlena nodded. "It sounds hungry." She shivered. "I don't think I like it."

Setting down his lamp, Norman leaned over and drew

175

the blankets closer about her shoulders before sitting down on the edge of the bed. "I know," he agreed. "Sometimes the wind gets rather fierce this time of year. I think it's complaining because it had to leave the mountains." He smiled down at her. "But Sis, we know who made the wind and who calms the storms. There is no need to be afraid. Just try to go back to sleep." He rose.

"Norman, please, won't you stay with me until I do fall asleep?" Orlena's voice sounded timid and, remembering that this was her first winter out on the ranch, he nodded.

"But I need to check on Mr. Davis. Then I'll be back. I'll light your lamp if you wish."

"Please do. It doesn't seem so bad when there is a light."

Once the dim glow of the second lamp cast a light on the bed, Norman, taking his own lamp, slipped from the room. He thought of asking Jenelle to sit with Orlena, but decided against it. "She needs to rest," he thought.

When he reached the sick man's room, he could hear coughing and quickly entered. Placing his lamp on the dressing table, Norman immediately poured a spoonful of cough syrup. "Here, Davis," he urged calmly, gently raising the man's head. "Swallow this and see if it will help."

The man did as he was told, but it was only after several minutes and several drinks of water that the cough subsided, and he lay back exhausted.

With the skilled touch of someone who had done the same thing many times before, Norman wiped the beads of perspiration from the older man's face. "Do you think you can sleep now?" he asked softly.

Davis nodded, his eyes already closed.

After straightening the blankets and making sure no cold draft was blowing on the bed, Norman picked up his lamp and moved quietly from the room.

When he reentered Orlena's room, he discovered her already sound asleep again. Blowing out her lamp, he continued his check of the upper rooms before moving downstairs. Everything was as it should be. He couldn't see any lights in the bunk house, but he wasn't even sure he could see the bunk house had it been daylight. As he mounted the stairs he wondered how the cattle were doing out in the storm. "I'll be glad when spring comes," he thought. "But then things will be very busy with all that comes with spring. A rancher never does get many days to just relax. But I wouldn't trade this life for any other one offered me!"

As he climbed back into bed, Jenelle turned over and murmured sleepily, "What took you so long?"

"Orlena was awake and a little frightened by the sound of the wind, and Davis was coughing. They're both asleep again now."

There was no reply, and Norman heard his wife's steady, even breathing and knew she probably hadn't even heard his reply. He smiled to himself in the darkness before closing his eyes.

In the morning the storm had nearly spent itself, with only occasional strong gusts of wind remaining to swirl the snow into the face of any who ventured out, as though trying to make the most of its expulsion from the mountains in the west. The snow had stopped falling and the sun was braving the bitter wind, trying to offer what warmth it could while the clouds were dancing in front of its face.

Norman, concerned for his cattle after the fierceness of the night's storm, headed out with his hands after breakfast to check on them. The horses, seemingly delighted to be out, pranced and tossed their heads in the brisk morning air as they waited for their riders to mount.

"You want me to let the rest of the horses out in the pasture, Mr. Mavrich?" Scott asked. "They're acting a bit upset that they weren't chosen to be ridden today."

After glancing up at the sky above and over towards the northwest, Norman nodded, "Sure, let them out. I think the wind will die down before long and it will probably clear up. I don't imagine we'll be gone too long, but even if we are, they should be fine. Hearter, Alden, Tracy, go give him a hand. The rest of us will start off." The men named hurried back to the barn and Norman called, "Burns, you have that sled hitched up yet?"

"Yes sir. She's ready to go," Burns called back from the sled they used to transport hay and supplies when checking on the cattle in the winter.

"All right then, Hardrich, St. John, let's head out."

Captain snorted and stepped forward eagerly as Norman swung onto his broad back. "Yes, boy, we're going now," he chuckled. "You're just as anxious to be off as I am, huh?"

The ride through the snow was enjoyable for all. The horses soon settled down and moved steadily forward, picking their way through the lowest drifts and avoiding the large mounds of snow. It was a little over an hour before the first of the cattle were reached. These appeared to be fine though their hay had been covered by the storm of the night before. Quickly the men shoveled away the snow and the cattle were soon busy with their breakfast.

It was before they left the first group of cattle that Scott, Alden, Hearter and Tracy caught up with them.

"You get all the horses out?" Hardrich asked as they rode up.

Scott nodded. "They all seemed mighty pleased with the arrangement too."

Norman remounted Captain. "Well, let's get on with things. There are other cattle to check."

It was several hours before Mr. Mavrich and his ranch hands were able to turn back, having checked on the last of the cattle. It had taken longer than Norman had thought it would but life on a ranch was often like that. No one seemed to mind the extra time, for the sun had chased the rest of the clouds away and the air was calm, even pleasant. Several of the hands had loosened their heavy coats.

"I wonder how many more snowstorms we'll be gettin' before spring comes," Alden mused as the men rode through the glittering fields of white.

"What's the almanac say, Hardrich?" Lloyd turned and asked the foreman who was riding behind him.

Hardrich chuckled, "It doesn't say how many storms we'll be gettin' a year."

"But does it say spring will be early or late?" Lloyd persisted.

"Neither."

"Now what's that supposed to mean?" demanded Tracy with a puzzled frown.

"I think it means," Norman put in, "that spring will come when it gets here and not a day sooner or later."

The lighthearted bantering continued until they had reached the last hill before the buildings of the ranch could be seen. Suddenly Captain quickened his pace, his head tossing as he snorted and whinnied. Astonished at his usual steady mount, Norman quickly attempted to calm him.

"Whoa there, boy. Steady. Easy now." He gently pulled on the reins, but the horse ignored the tug and plunged forward. "Captain! What has gotten in to you? Whoa!" Norman's voice had grown firm, but it did no good, for Captain continued climbing the hill until he reached the very top. Then, with a snort, he stopped.

Norman looked out across the snowy land and groaned, shaking his head. His horse snorted again as though to say, "I knew something wasn't right, but you wouldn't listen."

"Scott!" Norman turned in the saddle and called down the hill to the others whose horses were taking the hill more slowly. "Who shut the gate after you put the horses out?"

"I did, sir," Scott called back. "What's wrong?"

Norman didn't say anything else until the other riders had also reached the ridge. A collective groan came from the men and Norman sighed, "Did you latch the gate?"

"I know I did, but how on earth—" Scott didn't finish his sentence.

For a full minute the owner of Triple Creek Ranch, his foreman and his hands sat in silence staring at the scene before them, not quite willing to believe it was true. Every horse on Triple Creek except for the ones being ridden at the moment were scattered about the ranch enjoying their freedom by frolicking in the snow.

"Well," Norman said, straightening his shoulders and pulling his hat down a little lower, "let's get on with it." He reached down and unfastened his rope, which always hung on his saddle when he was out riding on the ranch, and began to build a loop.

It was a lively time the cattlemen had for most of the horses, delighting in their new freedom, declined to be caught and led the men on merry chases through the vastly untouched, snow blanketed yards. At last a few of the older, more mature horses, tiring of the sport, allowed themselves to be caught and taken to the barn. There Norman ordered Scott to take charge of them and the others as they were brought in.

On turning Captain to once more resume the round-up, Norman was hailed from the porch of the house.

"Mr. Mavrich!"

Riding over, Norman saw Mack Davis standing on the porch.

"Davis, what are you doing out?" he demanded. "Get back in before your cough gets worse."

"I'm all right," Davis insisted. "I can help ya round them horses up. After all—" His cough interrupted him.

"You're not helping, Davis, and that's final. Now get inside. That's an order!" He added the last as the man hesitated a moment.

Right then Mrs. O'Connor opened the door and ordered briskly, "Inside with ye now, tis later on that ye can be tellin' Norman Mavrich all about it."

Shaking his head, Norman sighed and wheeled Captain, setting off once more to bring the horses in.

It was a long chase and over a hour was spent without much success, for the horses which remained were young and spirited while the mounts of the men were tired from a long day of plodding through the drifts. At last Lloyd rode over to

Norman.

"Mr. Mavrich, I think I know what's going on with the horses."

Heaving a deep sigh, Norman took his hat off and wiped his face on the sleeve of his coat. "What?" he asked, putting his hat back on.

"I think it's that new horse, Shad. He seems to be the ring leader and if we catch him, I'd say we'd have a better chance at the others."

Norman had also been noticing the new horse, but hadn't really taken the time to think about it. Young Hearter's words struck him as sensible. "Let's give it a try."

It was another ten minutes before Hearter, Alden, Burns and Norman had the new horse boxed in. Shad pranced and tossed his head, rearing and giving a loud whinny as though laughing at all the work he had caused. The men tried getting a rope around his neck but the horse was as elusive as a coyote and cleverly evaded them. Norman was about to dismount and try catching the horse from the ground when Scott walked up to him.

"Let me try, sir," he said. "He knows me." Without giving Norman time to reply, Scott slowly approached the dark horse. "Come on, boy," he called. "I think you've given them all a good run."

Swiftly the horse's ears swiveled towards Scott and he allowed him to approach and slip a halter on him. "I'll take him back to the barn," Scott called as he led the horse away.

With a shake of his head, Norman beckoned his men. "All right, let's get on with it."

Once Shad was taken to the barn, the rest of the horses seemed more willing to be caught, except for Minuet. She was as determined to remain away from capture as Norman was to return her to the barn. Dismounting, Norman handed Captain's reins to Hardrich and said, "Have the men all take care of the horses and start on the chores."

"Right. But what are you going to do?"

"Bring Minuet in."

"By yourself?" Hardrich looked down at the tired but determined face of the ranch boss and then at the distant figure of the young horse. He shook his head.

Norman was also looking at the horse. "No," he said slowly, "I think I know . . ." His voice died away and he handed his coiled rope to his foreman. "Take this too, will you. I won't need it."

Hardrich remained where he was for a minute watching Norman stride not towards the horse, but in the direction of the ranch house. A slow smile crossed his face. "Of course," he muttered, "why didn't we think of it sooner." Then he rode to the barn, calling the men.

In less than five minutes Norman was seen coming out of the house with Jenelle, and together they strolled up the lane, paying no attention to the chestnut standing like a statue watching their every move. As they came abreast of her, Jenelle turned her head and called gently, "Minuet, come on girl."

The horses ears swiveled to catch the soft sound of the voice. It was a voice she knew, one that she loved. Taking a couple steps forward, Minuet stopped.

"Come on girl," Jenelle coaxed again. "Come take a walk with us."

With a nicker, Minuet danced through the snow until she came to Jenelle's side.

"That's my girl," Jenelle praised, rubbing her face as Norman caught hold of the halter. "Let's get you back to all your friends in a nice warm barn."

Feeling a hand on her halter, Minuet tried to shake it off but Norman held on firmly. "Whoa there. Come on Minuet, it's time to settle down." The horse, hearing the firm tones, seemed to realize that play time was over and became once again the sweet, though spirited, young horse Mrs. Mavrich was so fond of.

Together the three walked back down the lane towards the barn, Jenelle's hand tucked in her husband's arm while his free hand held on to Minuet's halter. They didn't talk much but enjoyed the quietness of the late winter afternoon.

"Soon it will be spring," Jenelle whispered with a little sigh.

"Are you sad or happy about it?" Norman looked down at his wife's upturned face.

"A little of both, I think. I'm looking forward to the flowers and green grass, but not the long days when I won't see much of you." Her soft, blue eyes looked adoringly into the grey ones above her and without a word Norman bent and kissed her.

T

CHAPTER 23

SIGNS OF SPRING

Arriving at the barn, Norman declined Scott's offer to take care of Minuet for him. "No thanks, Scott. Were the other horses all right? Good. Then let's get the chores finished up." He turned to Jenelle. "I'll be in as soon as the chores are done," he promised.

Jenelle nodded and returned to the house.

When Norman came in later, supper was waiting to be served and after quickly washing up, he sat down with a sigh. He was tired and hungry and supper smelled good.

"Mr. Mavrich, I reckon I ought ta tell ya."

Norman looked up, a piece of bread in one hand and his fork in the other. "Tell me what, Davis?"

"How them horses got out."

Putting the bread in his mouth, Norman nodded. He'd like to know how his entire herd of horses got out of the pasture.

"Well, ya see, with Shad bein' the only real friend I had fer years, I spent a lot a time with him. An' he's a natural learner an' picked up jest 'bout any trick right quick. I reckon he were put out in that there pasture with the rest a them horses?"

"Yes. Go on."

"I figured as much. Ya see, Shad, he knows how ta open

reg'lar gates an' I 'spect he jest did that very thing and headed out, an' the other horses followed."

"Why on earth didn't you tell me he knew how to open gates?" Norman sighed wearily.

Davis thoughtfully chewed the large piece of meat he had just stuffed in his mouth. At last, after taking a drink, he said, "I reckon ya never asked an' I never thought of it 'till I heard them horses was out."

A slight smile crossed Norman's face. "I never thought I had to ask if a horse could open pasture gates. Can he open anything else?" After Davis shook his head, Norman gave a relieved sigh before helping himself to another piece of beef and a spoonful of potatoes.

"Were the cattle all right?" Jenelle asked several minutes later into the silence that had descended.

"Yep."

"Norman," Orlena asked, "do you think there will be any more storms this winter like we had last night?"

Shrugging, he answered, "I can't say for sure, but I think winter is on its way out. Oh, we might have a few more snowfalls, but I'm rather doubtful we'll get many more such storms as last night."

Orlena shivered at the remembrance. "Good. I didn't like that one."

"You didn't stay awake very long," he returned with a brotherly smile.

"No," the girl confessed, "but I dreamed I was lost in it."

"I'm glad you weren't!" Norman exclaimed. "It's not fun being lost in a snowstorm, let me tell you!"

"Were you ever lost in one, Norman?" Orlena questioned eagerly.

It was only after the dishes were washed and the kitchen cleaned up that Norman agreed to tell the story.

"I was seventeen when it happened. It was early winter and there hadn't been much snow yet. Only a few inches were on the ground and Uncle thought it would be a good idea to try bringing the herd in closer. I don't remember how many hands we had at that time, but we all saddled up and rode out. I was sent to one section with orders to keep riding till I came to Crystal Creek and then I was to follow that to the north boundary and head back to the barn, driving any cattle I found with me. It all seemed easy enough since there usually weren't many cattle in that area at that time of year. Everyone of us carried supplies for a few days just in case we got lost or had to remain out on the range longer than planned.

"I must have been out for several hours before it began to snow lightly. I wasn't worried and soon came to Crystal Creek." Norman paused to add more wood to the fire before settling back in his chair and continuing his story.

"I don't know when I first began to notice that the snow was growing worse and the wind had picked up, but I figured the best thing to do was to continue on my way. There was at least one line shack along the north fence line which we used during round-up, and I thought I could make it that far; then after the storm stopped, I'd head back. It wasn't difficult following the creek and I was young and hopeful. Carefully I tried to watch for the fence line, but it was difficult to see much in that storm. I began to grow tired and cold, for the wind was strong and bitter, the snow swirled around my horse, and had it not been for the creek, I wouldn't have had any idea which direction to go. As it was, I continued urging my horse on and he, brave fellow, tried to oblige, though I'm sure it wasn't easy.

"Well, to make a long story short, at last I realized that the creek had vanished and there had been no sign of a fence anywhere. My horse stopped and refused to go any farther. Stiffly I slid from his back and almost fell when I tried to stand up, my legs were so stiff with the cold. For several minutes I tried to bring back warmth to my numb limbs. I had to have shelter. Packing the snow, I began to form a small shelter hoping to keep out some of the wind. Somehow I managed to build a lean-to large enough for my horse and me to crowd into, though there was no roof.

"It was then that I remembered the blanket tied to the saddle. This I managed to cut loose, for my fingers were too numb to untie the frozen thongs. I'm not sure how I managed, but somehow I was able to spread that blanket over the top of the wall and then I crawled under my horse and huddled in my coat."

"Why didn't you build a fire?" Orlena asked, wide-eyed and somewhat breathless. "And didn't you eat?"

Norman shrugged. "There wasn't anything to burn or no doubt I would have tried, and right then I was too tired to think of eating," he confessed. "All I cared about was sleep, so I curled up and let my eyes close.

"I don't know how long I slept, but I remember waking up stiff and cold. I heard my horse moving above me, but I couldn't tell if the storm had stopped or not. Nothing seemed to matter then and I must have fallen asleep again.

"It was some time later that I was finally aroused by my horse. He kept nudging me until I sat up and talked to him. The storm had stopped, and when I crawled out and shakily stood up, all I could see around me was snow. I had no idea where I was and nothing looked familiar. I didn't really want to leave my little shelter, but I knew I needed to get back to the ranch or Uncle would worry.

"My horse seemed more than willing to move on but it was with difficulty that I mounted him. I started in the direction I thought was home, but the horse refused to move. At last I just told him to go home and he started off in a completely different way.

"I don't really remember how long I rode, but I remember hearing voices and knowing that someone had found me.

"I'm not really clear on what happened after that," Norman recalled thoughtfully, gazing into the flames and falling silent.

"We know you were rescued, Norman," Jenelle said softly, "but how did it happen and where were you?"

"Huh?" Norman started from his reverie. "Oh, yes. The

storm lasted most of the night, and in the morning when I didn't come in with the rest of the men, Uncle got worried and the men all set out to try and find me. They naturally started the search along the route I was supposed to take, but didn't find any sign of me. Then, just before everyone split up to search in separate directions, one of the men spied my horse on the wrong side of the fence."

"How did you get there?" Davis asked

"The fence by Crystal Creek was down and in the storm I hadn't been able to see it. Well, they got me back to the house and it was weeks before Doc let me leave it."

"'Tis a rough life out here on a ranch entirely," Mrs. O'Connor exclaimed, shaking her head at Norman's story.

Spring was certainly on her way in, for each day the snow melted a little bit more and the sun shone most days. There were still a few days when a gentle snow would fall, but it never lasted long and the winds were more from the south. Everyone was feeling cabin fever, and coming back from school Orlena would report how much the snow had melted along the roads.

At last the day came when Norman, springing up onto the porch, called as he flung open the door, "Jenelle! Orlena! Mrs. O'Connor!"

The ladies hurried to the kitchen wondering what the excitement was. "Norman, what has happened?" Jenelle demanded.

"It's here!" he exclaimed, catching his wife in his arms and swinging her in a circle while she clung laughing but wholly mystified, to his neck. Setting her down, he caught her hand and pulled her down the porch steps calling over his shoulder, "Come and see!"

Wondering if her steady, dependable brother had lost his mind, Orlena followed with Mrs. O'Connor through the slushy snow to a bare patch of earth where no shading tree or tall grass had prevented the sun's warm rays.

Squatting down, Norman pointed. "See, Jenelle, the first crocus."

"Oh!" Unable to say another word for a minute, Jenelle dropped down beside her husband and, reaching out a gentle hand, softly touched the leaves of the daring little flower. "Spring," she whispered at last. "Spring."

It had at last arrived, and every day Jenelle and Orlena watched the growing patches of ground for signs of little green shoots to indicate the brave little flowers who pushed up their bright heads before the snow was completely gone.

One night Orlena woke to a sound she hadn't heard all winter, the sound of raindrops hitting her windowpane. Minding not that it was still very early in the morning, she slipped from her bed and hurried to the window, where she pressed her face against the cool glass and tried to see out into the dark. "This will melt the last of that tiresome snow," she thought, more delighted than she had ever been with spring's first rain.

By morning the last of the snow had disappeared and the rain ceased to fall, leaving only very muddy ground. For days mud seemed to be everywhere. The sun tried its best to dry up the ground, but after so much snow it was a slow job. Mrs. O'Connor sighed at the muddy footprints on the porch. Mud got tracked into the house when Orlena fed the chickens or arrived home from school; it came in when Norman brought the milk, did the chores or just came inside for meals; even Jenelle brought it in with her when she ventured outside to look at the flowers or to hang out the wash. At last, throwing up her hands in surrender, Mrs. O'Connor exclaimed, "It's impossible indeed! It's well I might try an' stop everyone from going out the door entirely!"

"Is it the mud, Mrs. O'Connor?" asked Jenelle sympathetically. "I gave up long ago. My mother used to tell me that 'come the first days of spring and all the snow melts and the rains come, expect the house to be well tracked with mud.' Then she'd say that once it dried it would sweep up well."

"But Deary," Mrs. O'Connor protested, "there's never a chance for it to dry, for someone always brings in more."

A merry laugh rang out in the kitchen as Jenelle sank down onto a chair. "Oh, I know! Let's just do what my mother did. We'll sweep the floor only after everyone is in for the night and then at least it will stay clean until morning." She laughed again, knowing how hard mud was to keep out of any ranch house in the spring.

"I don't see but that's what we'll have to be doing indeed, but tis a right pity a house can't be kept clean in this country."

"But Mrs. O'Connor," protested Jenelle warmly, "you've kept the house wonderfully clean all through the winter and, in fact, ever since you arrived the house has been shining. A little mud won't hurt us now."

With a sad shake of her head, the housekeeper turned to the stove and added a few sticks of wood. She had been preparing to bake bread when the sight of more mud coming in on Norman's boots had brought on her outburst.

Jenelle watched the busy hands and sighed, remembering how tired she had been before Norman had brought Mrs. O'Connor from the city to live with them. Now she didn't know what she would do without her.

T

CHAPTER 24

WINTER'S LAST FLING

Norman came in from the pasture a few days later with the news that the first cow had dropped her calf. "A fine heifer too," he said, hanging up his hat. "Hardrich said he figures we'll have at least a dozen more calves before the end of the week."

"Did Mr. Davis go out with you today?" Orlena questioned as the family seated themselves at the supper table. Mack Davis had moved out to the bunk house with the men as soon as the warmer weather had arrived.

Norman nodded and then bowed his head to ask the blessing on the meal.

When supper was nearly over, Norman, having told about his day out among the cattle, turned to his sister and asked, "How was your day at school?"

"Miss Hearter changed my seat. Now Charity and I share a desk, and I don't have to sit across the aisle from Elvira." There was no hiding the eagerness in Orlena's voice when she talked about her new seat-mate and Jenelle was glad.

Leaning back in his chair, Norman nodded, well pleased. "Perhaps Hearter can bring his sister out here some Saturday. And by the way," he paused, smiling while he waited for Orlena's exclamations of delight to end. "How are you and Elvira getting along?"

"We aren't."

Raising his eyebrows and looking keenly at his sister, he questioned, "Why not?"

Orlena shrugged. "She hasn't spoken to me since the fight. And yes," she hastened to add, seeing her brother was about to speak, "I have tried to be nice to her and invited her to eat lunch with some of the other girls, but she acts like I don't even exist."

"Keep trying and doing your part," Norman admonished. "I know it's not always easy, but don't give up."

"All right," was the somewhat reluctant reply. Orlena would much rather have forgotten the existence of Elvira Ledford altogether, for it was tiring and humiliating to have her overtures of friendship so constantly ignored.

T

Hardrich's predictions about the calves came true, and before Saturday a dozen new calves were out on the range.

When Orlena came home from school Friday afternoon, her brother was waiting for her in the yard. "Hurry inside and change. I'll have Anything saddled by the time you get back."

An anxious look crossed Orlena's face. "S . . . saddled?" she stammered. "Wh . . . why? What are we going to do?"

"I'm going to give you your first riding lesson." Norman grinned and gently tugged one of her ringlets.

"I . . . I . . . I don't—"

Norman gave her no time to finish. "Hurry up now. We don't have a lot of time until I'll be too busy to help you. Scoot!"

Orlena hurried into the house, her face a mixture of fright and excitement. "Jenelle," she wailed, when she caught sight of her sister in the upper hall. "Norman said he's going to teach me to ride now, and I don't think I want to!"

"Of course you do," Jenelle smiled. "Norman's a good teacher, and before you know it you'll be riding to school and all over the ranch. Why you could even bring Charity home

from school with you sometimes if you could ride a horse."
As she had talked, she had hurried Orlena into her room,
taken the school books from her, and pulled a dress suitable
for riding from the closet. "Quickly now," she urged briskly.
"You don't want to keep Norman waiting."

"Will you come out too?" Orlena asked as Jenelle almost
pushed her from the room moments later.

"I can for a few minutes, but then I must work on
supper. Mrs. O'Connor was feeling tired this afternoon after
spring cleaning the kitchen and is lying down, so I'm
preparing supper."

Norman was a good teacher, as Orlena quickly
discovered. He wasn't impatient, but he insisted that she do
things right. Before long Orlena was sitting on Anything's
back, her feet in the stirrups, trying to remember how to hold
the reins. Norman had already led her around the corral
several times until Orlena began to feel confident in the older
horse's steady, plodding movements.

"Norman," she asked suddenly, "how did she get such a
funny name?"

"The horse? Well, you see," and Norman pushed his hat
back and leaned an elbow on the fence rail while hooking the
thumb of his other hand onto his belt. "When she was born,
Hardrich, who was mighty young back then and not the
foreman, went to Uncle and asked what he wanted to name
the filly. Uncle was busy with other things and waving his
hand he replied, 'Oh, I don't know, name her anything.' And
she's been called that ever since."

Orlena giggled. She would like to name a horse someday.
What would she call it? Princess? Lady Marian? Perhaps she
should think of something more original like— She was
startled from her thoughts by her brother's hand on her knee.

"Wake up, Sis."

Blinking, she looked down.

"Walk Anything around the corral by yourself," he
directed when he had her attention.

It wasn't until Orlena was on her second time around the

corral that she realized with a start that she, Orlena Mavrich, was riding a horse by herself on Triple Creek Ranch, and she wasn't afraid.

As Jenelle watched the flushed face and sparkling eyes of the girl before her and listened to her excited account of riding all by herself, she thought back to the first full day Orlena had spent on the ranch. The two pictures were a sharp contrast and Jenelle gave an involuntary smile of approval at the bright and eager person talking so happily in the kitchen.

"And Norman says he'll give me another lesson tomorrow and another on Monday! I didn't dream riding would be so enjoyable! But," she added with a half frightened look, "I don't think I want to ride Minuet."

"Don't worry, you won't." It was Norman who had just entered the kitchen. "You'll be riding Anything until I think you're ready for something with a little more speed." He smiled down at his sister, kissed his wife and left to get an arm load of wood for the kitchen stove.

"Jenelle, when did you learn to ride?"

"Me? I don't recall not knowing how," Jenelle confessed. "My father and brothers had me riding with them in the saddle before I could talk plainly and would often lead me around the yards for what seemed like hours at the time."

Orlena sighed. "Norman said that someday I'll be able to ride as well as you. But I've never seen you ride."

Jenelle laughed. "And you won't see it now. Set the table, please."

It was Monday morning and Norman had just finished breakfast and stood looking out the open kitchen door at the clouds in the sky. The sun was trying to come up, but it was having difficulty peeking through the bank of clouds which seemed to rim the ranch and the entire surrounding area.

When a sudden cool breeze struck Norman in the face, he started, his eyes turning towards the northwest. Suddenly he snatched up his hat and raced towards the bunkhouse.

Jerking open the door he discovered the men still at the table eating. They looked up in astonishment as Mr. Mavrich burst into the room. "Hardrich, come out and look at this and tell me if it's what I think it is," he ordered quickly.

At once Hardrich shoved back his chair and followed the visibly excited ranch boss out into the yard while the other men, curious about what could be so important to warrant Mr. Mavrich's strange behavior, followed the two older men outside.

Norman was pointing to the far northwest where low clouds were gathering near the distant mountain peaks. Scratching his head, the foreman nodded, "Yep, I reckon we're in for a late snowstorm."

With a groan, Norman said, "That's what I was afraid of." For a moment he stood staring out at the clouds. Then, half to himself, he began talking. "Unless the wind changes it ought not to hit for a few hours at least. That should give nearly enough time to round up the stray cows and make sure the calves are in shelter. Of course if the wind does change . . . it'll be a gamble either way." He turned and noticed the men gathered around watching the clouds and waiting. "All right men, you know what's coming." His voice was brisk and firm. He began issuing orders. "First off every one get his coat and be ready for a day in the saddle. Scott, start saddling up the horses, and get out a string of 'em to take along. We may need to switch out mounts. Burns, hitch up the light wagon and load it with hay. If that storm sticks around, the cattle are going to need it. St. John, get out rations for each of us for two days. Hopefully we won't need them but there's no telling how long this storm is going to last. Hearter, get the saddlebags for St. John then give Burns a hand loading the hay. Tracy, get the blankets and tie a bedroll behind each saddle then give Scott a hand. Alden, get any supplies we may need out on the range during a blizzard and load 'em on

Giant. Davis," here he hesitated just a moment. "I don't want to leave the ladies here alone without a man around. I'm going to leave you in charge here. That means you'll have to take care of all the chores until we return."

Mack Davis met the steady grey eyes leveled at him with a straight look in return and nodded. "Yes, sir. I reckon I can take care a things round here till ya git back."

"Good." Norman turned to his foreman. "Hardrich, come with me, and we'll make plans. I have to let Jenelle know what's happening."

In less than an hour the men were in the saddle and ready to move out. Jenelle and Mrs. O'Connor stood on the porch and watched them. Mrs. Mavrich knew how hard these spring snowstorms could be on new calves and it would be a hardship to lose even a few of them. Norman shouted something and they were off, heading for the pastures where the cattle would be scattered far and wide, enjoying the new spring grass unless they too sensed the coming storm.

Jenelle had assured her husband when he told her the news of the coming storm and their plans, not to worry about her or the rest of the ranch. "We'll be fine. Davis will look after things, don't worry." Now that they were gone, however, Jenelle leaned against a post on the porch and sighed. What was winter's last fling going to be like? How long would it last? Perhaps it would all blow over with only a few flakes.

Urging Captain to a steady, though rapid pace, Norman led his men across the fields heading towards the vast open range beyond, where his cattle grazed. In less than an hour they found the first cows and, spreading out, began to search for the rest, especially those who could give birth at any time or already had a calf. Slowly, a few at a time, cows were found and herded together in a sheltered place. Then the snow began to fall. It wasn't heavy, but it was steady with large, fat flakes.

"Mavrich," Alden called as Norman came up to the herd

leading his horse. "We're still missing a dozen cows that should be here and three of them have calves."

Norman nodded. "Scott," he called, seeing his wrangler saddling a new horse for Hearter.

Handing the reins to Lloyd, Scott, pulling his hat lower, hurried around the herd to Norman.

"See what you can do for Apache, he's strongly favoring his right foreleg." As Scott ran his experienced hands over the horse's leg, Norman asked, "Is Captain rested enough to go out again?"

"Sure. You could probably ride that horse all day without tiring him too much," Scott glanced up to say.

Quickly Norman transferred his saddle from Apache to Captain who seemed eager to be off again, then, leaving Scott to care for Apache, he started off once more in search of the last few cows. Hearter joined him before he had gotten very far.

"When I was bringing those last few cows in," the young hand said, "I crossed the top of that hill yonder," and he pointed. "I thought I might have heard something coming from across the ravine. Think any of the cows we're looking for would have gone over there?"

"Could have. Let's take a look. The rest of the nearby area has been pretty well searched." The snow was growing heavier as the ranch boss and his youngest hand turned their horses' heads into the wind and headed for a distant hill. There was no way a horse could cross the ravine from the hill; they would have to go around and cross Penny Creek and climb the hill there.

The wind had picked up and both riders turned their collars up and pulled their hats down.

"You know," Norman had to speak loudly to be heard above the wind and through the folds of his bandana which he had tied about his face. "Quite a few years ago we had one cow that decided for some strange reason that the plateau where we're heading was her favorite place. We could always find her there and it always took some effort to get her down and back with the herd. But we sold that cow a couple years back."

"Maybe we have another one who likes it," Lloyd laughed.

"I hope not!"

Reaching the creek, the men urged their horses through the cold water and up onto the other side. Norman was just glad that the creek hadn't started to freeze yet. It was a cold climb up the hill. The snow was already several inches deep and it was hard to tell when it would stop falling.

Suddenly Captain's ears swiveled forward. "Do you hear something, boy?" Norman asked, straining his own ears to listen.

CHAPTER 25

A NEW DAY

For several silent minutes they continued upward. At last the plateau was reached and, sure enough, there was one of the missing cows and her calf. The calf was covered with snow and shaking.

Lloyd at once sprang off his horse, untied the blanket from behind his saddle and moved to the calf's side. There he gently rubbed it with the blanket trying to dry it. "There's no way this little thing is going to be able to walk all the way back," he looked up to say.

"You can carry it back on the horse. Try to keep it warm and it might survive."

"What about the mother?"

Norman had been eyeing the cow who didn't seem too interested in her baby at the moment. "If she won't follow you, we'll fix a halter with your rope and you can drag her back if need be. Once you get started I'll keep looking."

Lloyd nodded and, without a word, scooped the shivering calf up and returned to his horse. Even when her baby was taken away, the cow seemed indifferent and quickly Norman, taking Lloyd's rope, fixed a halter for the cow and handed the other end to Lloyd. "Keep her up with you," he directed. "Perhaps she'll bond with her calf when you get back to the herd."

Lloyd nodded and set off. The wind was dying down but

the snow continued to fall.

Starting across the plateau and down the other side, Norman strained his eyes and ears for any sign or sound of a cow. At last his searching was rewarded by two standing together under a solitary tree. Neither one was inclined to leave their meager shelter, but Norman, not knowing how long the storm would last, drove them on. They bawled when they crossed the creek and bawled as they rounded a hill, but Captain kept up such a steady pace behind them and Norman paid so little attention to their protests, that they could do nothing but continue on.

At last the rest of the herd was reached and Norman found most of his men gathered beside a fire in a makeshift shelter. As he rode up, Scott hurried over to take Captain's reins. "Is everyone back, Scott?"

"Yes, sir. Alden and Tracy are patrolling the cattle now. Everyone else is eating and warming up."

Yielding Captain's reins to Scott, Norman tramped over to the fire. There he found Lloyd still with the calf. "Wouldn't she take him back?"

Lloyd shook his head. "No, not yet. Hardrich suggested I warm him up a while and then try again."

Sitting down on a log, Mr. Mavrich accepted the steaming plate of beans St. John held out to him. "Did we get them all?"

Hardrich shook his head. "No, there's still one cow missing."

"Which one?"

"The first to drop her calf this year. The men needed to eat and warm up, then we're going out again."

It wasn't until he had finished his beans and drunk a cup of coffee that Norman spoke again. "Have Alden and Tracy eaten? Then two of you men stay here to relieve them in another hour. The rest of us had better saddle up and start out again."

He had been riding for over an hour, trying to think of

where the cow might have gone and wondering if perhaps she had already been found. He hadn't heard any shots, but perhaps he was too far away and the snow had muffled them. Just as Norman was about to turn and head back to the herd, Captain stopped short and snorted. "What is it, Boy?" Lifting his lantern high, Norman peered through the falling snow.

Then he heard it. A faint yet mournful bawling. "Come on, boy," Norman urged. "Let's help her."

Obligingly, the horse moved forward several yards and once again stopped. Knowing that his horse must have a reason for not advancing, Norman dismounted and cautiously moved forward, holding his lantern high.

"Oh, so that's the trouble, is it?" he muttered. All the melting snow had created a small gully, and down in the bottom was a calf. Up above, on the opposite side, was the mama cow, bawling for her baby. "All right, Captain," Norman spoke to his horse. "Let's get the calf up first and then see if we can't find a place for Mrs. Cow to cross over and join us."

It was the work of a good quarter of an hour before Norman had the calf up on level ground again, and the whole time he was working the mama cow bawled. Finding a place for the cow to cross over wasn't easy, but at last Norman found it, though he had to cross it first and drive the cow across by firing two shots in the air.

Together at last, the cow stopped bawling and calmly plodded along beside Norman's horse on which her baby was slung.

Hunching himself over the calf to try and protect it from the cold flakes which continued to fall from the dark night sky, with his hat low, his bandana over the lower part of his face and his lit lantern hanging from the saddle, Norman allowed Captain to pick his own way through the snow towards the camp and herd. Knowing that the cow wouldn't stray far from her calf, Norman hadn't bothered tying her to the saddle.

It was a long, cold night the men spent out in the snow with the herd. Two of the cows dropped their calves during the night and had to be brought closer to the fire to keep the babies warm. Thankfully the snow stopped before midnight, and before dawn the clouds had nearly all slipped away as though to let the sun see the mischief they had been up to.

When Orlena woke that morning, she stared gloomily out her window. Snow, everywhere. She was sick of snow. Why had it suddenly turned cold and snowed again? Wasn't spring really here? It never snowed after spring arrived in the city! Pulling on her warm clothes, and still grumbling, she hurried downstairs.

"Where's Norman?" she demanded as soon as she caught sight of Jenelle.

"Still out with the cattle. Hopefully the sun will melt the snow and he and the men will be able to come home today."

Slapping the spoons on the table, she complained, "He was supposed to give me another riding lesson yesterday and now he isn't even home today!"

Jenelle, who hadn't slept well, replied quietly, "I know he'll give you another lesson as soon as he can. Now, finish setting the table. Mr. Davis should be in shortly and you have school."

Orlena didn't want to go to school in the snow again and a pout came over her face.

Breakfast was eaten in complete silence on Orlena's part and as soon as she was finished, she went up to her room to get her books. Spying her Bible on the table next to her bed, she gave a sigh and picked it up. She had neglected to read it that morning, the sight of the white world outside having taken her thoughts elsewhere. Flipping it open at random, she read the first verse her eyes saw. Then she read it a second time.

"A merry heart doeth good like a medicine," she mused thoughtfully. "But I don't want to be merry or happy," she frowned, sitting down on the edge of her bed. "I don't even feel like smiling." Right then something Mrs. O'Connor had said to her just the other day came back. "Tis easy to be cheerful when things are going yer way, but ye can't be cheerful without the Good Lord to help when yer mind is all tangled up an' ye feel only like frownin'." For a moment Orlena sat and thought soberly. Did she want to go through the day trying to be good in her own strength? Slowly she slipped from the bed to her knees.

"Lord Jesus, I don't want to be happy this morning, but I know I should. Please help me to put a smile on today. For Jesus sake, Amen."

Rising, she gently shut the Bible and placed it back on the table. Then, gathering up her schoolbooks, she left her room. "Jenelle looked like she could use something to cheer her up. I'll try to smile as I leave."

She practiced as she went downstairs, again as she pulled on her coat and slipped on her rubbers. By the time she was ready to depart, a smile came readily to her lips and she called out cheerily, "Good bye, Jenelle!"

Smiling in return, Jenelle dropped a kiss on Orlena's cheek as she said, "Have a good day in school. Hopefully the snow will melt soon and you can ride again."

The sun shone brightly all morning, and by noon much of the snow was gone and patches of very damp grass could be seen. It was late afternoon, and nearly all the snow had melted except for in a few shady places on the north side of the ranch buildings, when the sound of horses approaching brought Jenelle out to the kitchen door. Tired and muddy, the eight cowboys came riding in to the yard.

"Norman!" Jenelle cried, flinging a shawl about her shoulders and hurrying out to welcome him.

Catching sight of her, Norman reined in Captain and swung off to greet her. "Are you all right?" he asked as she clung to him a minute.

"Yes, I'm just glad you're back."

"I'm glad too. Lord willing, that was the last snowstorm of the season."

T

It was the last snowfall and within a few days all traces of winter's last fling had vanished. Everywhere the grass was turning green, trees were bursting into blossom and new life was beginning to make itself felt.

As the days passed, Norman made sure his sister learned how to ride a horse. If he had no time, one of the other men, usually Hardrich or Alden, instructed her, and she was delighted when her brother allowed her to ride into town with him one Saturday morning for a few supplies which Jenelle had forgotten. On the return to the ranch Orlena turned to Norman with a question.

"Do you think," she began, "that I could ride Anything to school on Monday?"

For a moment Norman eyed her critically. "I don't see why not, unless it's raining."

Orlena gave a squeal of excitement and Anything, startled out of her usual calm, broke into a ragged canter. "Help!" Orlena cried out, grasping the saddle horn and forgetting about the reins entirely.

As soon as Anything started off, Norman had nudged Captain into a pace which matched that of the frightened horse. Riding beside his sister, Norman's calm, though slightly amused, voice reached her ears. "Pick up your reins and slow her down."

"How?" she gasped, afraid to let go of the secure saddle horn.

Before Norman could reply, Anything, deciding that whatever had startled her must have been left far behind, slowed down of her own accord and turned her head to see what had become of her rider.

"Oh, she's not running away," Orlena sighed with relief,

venturing to sit straight and pick up the reins. "Why didn't you stop her?" she demanded. "I could have fallen off."

"I didn't need to stop her, you're the one who scared her," Norman replied. "If you can't check and calm a horse after you've scared her, perhaps you aren't ready to ride in to school."

At that Orlena promised that she would always be careful not to scare Anything.

"All right," Norman consented. "But you'll have to make sure you come directly home after school or Jenelle will worry."

Orlena again promised.

Before much more could be said, dust from a quickly ridden horse was seen. It was Mr. Bates from the Rising B. On seeing them, he pulled up and asked excitedly, "Mavrich, have you had any cattle rustlers on your place?"

"Rustlers?" Norman exclaimed in surprise. "No, I can't say that I have. Why?"

"Well, we were hit last night," Bates replied. "My boys and I followed them to the road and then lost the trail. I'm ridin' into town to get the sheriff."

Norman thought Bates ought to have sent for the sheriff at once but refrained from saying so. "Do you know of any other ranches they might have tried?"

Bates shook his head. "Haven't had time to ask around. You'd best keep an eye open though. There's no tellin' when they'll strike again."

Norman nodded. "We'll do that. Thanks,"

Mr. Bates nodded and touched his hat quickly to Orlena. "Well, I must be off. Good day, Mavrich."

After turning to watch the man ride off, Orlena frowned. Looking up at her brother she asked, "Rustlers?"

He sighed. "Cattle thieves. We haven't had any in these parts for several years." He shook his head and urged Captain forward.

Ⓣ

The sun was barely above the horizon while the sky, still glowing with gold, pink and orange changing into purple and blue, held one or two last brave stars like sparkling diamond pins holding up the darker canvas of heaven until the king of day should rise high enough to claim it. The air was calm and still, and the morning songs of several birds seemed extra sweet as the family and hands of Triple Creek climbed into the waiting carriage and wagon. The drivers clicked to horses and they set off for town. It was Easter morning. There had been a dew in the early dawn and everywhere the drops of moisture sparkled and flashed in the rays of the rising sun.

The small church was filled with people that Sunday morning and the message the minister preached rang with triumph and life. "Christ indeed is alive," his strong voice sounded to the farthest corners of the room. "He has conquered Satan, He has conquered sin and He has conquered death. Why did Jesus Christ die a cruel death on the cross? Because He loved each one of us. Because He wanted us to have fellowship with His Father, to spend eternity with Him. That is why He died. And He snatched the victory from the grave when He arose triumphant, having taken the sting away from death for those who believe in Him. This is the rest of the Christmas story. The reason Jesus came to this earth. What a glorious reason we, who believe in Him, have to celebrate!"

Orlena had never listened to an Easter sermon with such a feeling of wonder and awe as she did that morning. Her sins were gone and she was one of those who could celebrate.

Coming out of the church after the service was over, Norman found himself waiting in the aisle with Elbert Ledford of the Bar X. After shaking hands with the young man warmly, Norman asked, "It's good to see you again. How have things been over at the Bar X?"

Elbert nodded. "All right as far as the cattle business

goes."

"And the family life?" Norman pressed, noting that no one else of the family was present.

"Not so well, I'm afraid. Mr. Mavrich, I keep praying, but things don't seem to be getting better, they seem worse."

Stepping aside to let others pass, Norman spoke earnestly, "Remember, Elbert, that when it's the darkest, the smallest light shines the brightest. Are you the only praying one in your family?"

"I know Mother prays, but I don't think anyone else does."

Mr. Mavrich placed a hand on the young man's shoulder. "Never forget the promise that where two or more are gathered, there He is with you. It may take a while, but don't give up." He was thinking of his own sister and the long struggle it had been before she gave herself up to the Lord. "I'll be praying for you, and if you ever need to talk, just ride over."

"Thank you, sir," Elbert said gratefully. "With the sermon and now your encouragement, I think I'm ready to face life again."

The two men shook hands and moved down the aisle.

Norman was quiet on the drive home. He couldn't help but wonder about the Bar X and the Ledford family. He never known them very well, but for some reason they seemed destined to cross his path.

When the carriage reached the top of a hill, Orlena looked down and saw Triple Creek Ranch spreading out before her. She remembered her first sight of it. Then it was summer, now it was Easter, and so much had happened in between. Glancing at her brother and Jenelle, she gave a slight sigh. She could hear some of the men talking in the wagon behind their carriage and she turned to see them. Lloyd Hearter was driving and a slight smile touched the girl's lips as she recalled their first meeting. "I was such a brat," she thought. Beside her sat Mrs. O'Connor; steady, imperturbable

Mrs. O'Connor, with capable hands and an Irish lilt to her speech.

The house and barn came into view and a whinny from Minuet in the corral welcomed them home. "Home," thought Orlena, glancing around. "Yes, I am home." She allowed her brother to help her from the carriage and paused to look about, as though seeing the ranch with new eyes. "I wonder what the rest of spring and summer will bring," she murmured to herself. She was eager and ready to find out.

T

And now, a sneak preview of Book Three in the
Triple Creek Ranch series:

"Mr. Mavrich!"

Norman Mavrich turned quickly from the corral as the shout and the sound of pounding hooves thundering down the lane alerted him to trouble. "That looks like Elbert Ledford from the Bar X!" he exclaimed to Jim Hardrich, the foreman of Triple Creek Ranch and Lloyd Hearter, the youngest hand. "Wonder what's gotten him so upset?"

There was no time for either man to reply before the excited rider had reined in his foam covered horse before them.

"What's wrong, Elbert?" Norman asked sharply, stepping up beside his visitor and noticing the young man's pale face and the rapid breathing of both horse and rider.

"It's Pa . . . rustlers . . . hands left . . . accused 'em . . . ranch . . . no one . . . cattle . . ."

"Whoa, slow down a bit there, Ledford. Now, just dismount, get a hold of yourself and then tell us what's going on. Here, Hearter," Mavrich directed, passing the reins of the exhausted horse to his ranch hand. "Take care of the horse."

Lloyd nodded and led the horse slowly towards the barn. He was curious to know what was going on at the Bar X but knew better than to argue with the ranch boss.

"Lloyd," a gentle voice called from the porch of the house. "Who just rode in?"

Lloyd looked up. "Elbert Ledford did, Mrs. Mavrich. He looks about done in too."

Jenelle Mavrich nodded and slipped inside.

Back at the corral, Elbert was slowly catching his breath and making a second attempt to tell his troubles. "We had rustlers at our place last night," he began, taking off his hat and running his fingers through his hair. "We found we were missing twenty-five head this morning."

Hardrich let out a whistle. "Twenty-five head in one night!"

"Well, I reckon it's been going on more than last night, but no one's had time to check. Pa got real angry over the whole thing. I've never seen him so worked up. Why he . . . he . . ." Elbert turned away and rested his elbows on the rail fence of the corral, his sentence unfinished.

Norman exchanged quick glances with Hardrich before placing a hand on the young man's shoulder. "What happened, Ledford?"

Elbert didn't turn around and his voice was low. "He accused the men of stealing the cattle themselves. Everyone denied it and then Pa fired our foreman and the others quit, except Cook. Pa collapsed right after that. Edgar and I were able to get him to bed. Now Edgar's gone for the doc and I . . . I didn't know who else to turn to, so—"

"You came to the right place, Elbert," Norman interrupted, squeezing his shoulder. "I'll ride back with you."

About the Illustrator

Nikola Belley is a self-taught artist, who enjoys exploring various mediums, from sketching to oil painting. A homeschool graduate, she is also a costume designer and seamstres and participates in international folk dance, music studies, and a myriad of family activities. Nikola lives in Missouri with her parents and eight siblings.

29916703R00127

Made in the USA
Charleston, SC
29 May 2014